THE B] UNWANTED SURROGATE

A BILLIONAIRE PREGNANCY

ROMANCE By..

LENA SKYE

This is a work of fiction. Similarities to real people, places or events are entirely coincidental.

Fancy A FREE BWWM Romance Book??

Join the "**Romance Recommended**" Mailing list today and gain access to an exclusive **FREE** classic BWWM Romance book along with many others more to come. You will also be kept up to date on the best book deals in the future on the hottest new BWWM Romances.

* Get FREE Romance Books For Your Kindle & Other Cool giveaways

* Discover Exclusive Deals & Discounts Before Anyone Else!

* Be The FIRST To Know about Hot New Releases From Your Favorite Authors

Click The Link Below To Access This Now!

Oh Yes! Sign Me Up To Romance
Recommended For FREE!

Already subscribed?

OK, Read On!

BOOK DESCRIPTION

Biology student River-Lea Thompson's plan to be a surrogate mother for a rich billionaire and his wife was meant to be her way out of her debt problems.

But she had no idea that her problems were only just beginning.

Just weeks away from giving birth and Silicon Valley billionaire Matthew Chase has told River-Lea that he and his wife have separated and as a result the terms of the agreement will have to be adjusted.

With Matthew's wife no longer interested in raising a baby with no connection to her, Matthew feels he has no choice but to suggest that he pay River-Lea to raise the baby for him.

Can she possibly accept the billionaire's outrageous proposal? Or might there be another way to solve this predicament...

ALSO...

***THIS LIMITED EDITION PACKAGE
ALSO INCLUDES
THE BELOW FREE BONUS BOOK!***

The Billionaire's Convenient Surrogate

Billionaire casino owner Parker Spesato was having a hard time finding a suitable surrogate to give him the child he has always wanted. Whilst at the same time Alexandria Frey was looking for a way out of her abusive relationship and was willing to do anything to make enough money to escape.

When Parker proposed that Alexandria be his surrogate mother it seemed to be an arrangement based more on convenience than perfection but it seems that both of them have nothing to lose but possibly everything to gain...

Table Of Contents

Chapter 5

Chapter 6

Chapter 7

THE BILLIONAIRE'S UNWANTED SURROGATE

Chapter One

The golden afternoon sun shone warmly through the windows of the brightly painted little beach house that looked out over the Pacific Ocean. Sitting on the deck of the house in a comfortable chaise lounge beneath a wide umbrella was a young woman who was laid back, eyes closed, fanning herself with a paper fan in her hand. There was a breeze coming in off of the glittering blue sea just down the little path from the house, but she liked the feel of the fanned air moving over her face.

She was of medium height, not much more than five and a half feet tall. Her skin was a caramel mocha color; the color that happens when coffee is made with just the right amount of cream in it. She had loose, finger-length curls all over her head, an oval-shaped face, and high rounded cheeks. Her full lips were slightly parted as she breathed in the fresh sea air and let it back out again slowly. She had blue eyes when they were open, much the same color as the water that was washing in to shore, hushing and shushing the sand it rolled over.

She lifted her free hand and placed it on her enormously rounded belly, rubbing her fingers back and forth on the skin soothingly. There was a strong bump from inside the skin, and River Lea Thompson smiled to herself as she rubbed the spot where she had been kicked, thinking of the little one inside of her, who might be playing, or who might be objecting to the warm day.

It was early July, and it felt like it to River Lea, and she was sure it felt like it to the baby inside of her. It was a peculiar circumstance about that baby. It wasn't her baby. River Lea was trying to find a way to pay for the remainder of her college education as a marine biologist, because she didn't want to graduate with debt. She had looked all over Santa Cruz for a good money opportunity and hadn't found one. She had even gone as far as Silicon Valley. Just a short drive up the highway, hoping to find a solution there, but there was nothing that was going to come close to meeting the financial goal she had in mind.

She'd been talking to her best friend, Gibby, and he mentioned that he'd heard of a medical clinic that was looking for young women to be surrogate mothers, and they were offering considerable payment for the service. She had laughed at first, but then the more she thought about it, the more it seemed like the perfect solution to her. Carry a baby for someone who couldn't have one; help them have a family, be able to go to school in the first six months of pregnancy and then have the summer off in time to have the baby before school started again, and then get into the new school year with no debt, a massive bank account, and a body healed from the birth.

The more she considered it, the better it sounded. She'd taken Gibby with her to go tour the clinic and talk with the doctors and he had supported her fully in the idea, so she signed the paperwork and waited for a call from the prospective parents.

The wait didn't take long, and she was surprised and relieved about that. The call came two weeks later, and she went to the clinic to meet the couple. The husband was an extraordinarily handsome man; over six feet tall with dark brown hair, warm brown eyes, and a jaw line that looked as if Michelangelo himself had chiseled it out of Italian marble. He was solid with muscle, but his demeanor and manner were soft. He had a pleasant way about him, as if he was most often unruffled, and ready to help anyone, whether it was to offer a smile or a hand.

His wife looked like a model who might have just flown in from France; she was six feet tall and slender with subtle curves. Her skin was darker than River Lea's, and her eyes were brown like her husband's. She was beautiful to look at, with her

13

long black hair that reached her thin waist and framed her fine features. She was polite, but she didn't seem to have the same warm pleasantness that her husband had.

River Lea wasn't too concerned with the woman's personality, though. What she was concerned with was the fact that the couple were billionaires and that they wanted her to carry a child for them, and they were offering her an extremely generous sum of money to do it. The husband, Matthew Chase, had offered River Lea twice what the clinic was asking, so that she could keep more money, and his wife Amil, though annoyed with him about the expense, was in agreement on the amount.

She met with the pair and they'd gotten along well enough that she agreed to take on their request and carry their child for them and give birth to it. She had timed it just right, and it had worked out. There wasn't much morning sickness for her and she had made it through the spring semester all right. Summer had come and she'd taken the time off of school to relax and make sure the pregnancy went well.

River Lea was eight months along, the baby was good, and she was almost finished with the deal. Then she would have time to heal and she could go back for her fall semester in a normal state and more than all the money she needed for school, and be able to graduate when she wanted to. She was looking forward to it with great anticipation.

The cell phone beside her on the table rang, and she opened her eyes and looked over at it. It was Gibby, her best friend. She smiled and reached for the phone, picking it up with a grin. "Hey there!" she greeted him.

"What are you doing?" he asked with a sly and curious tone.

She pushed herself up on the chaise lounge a little and took in a deep breath, looking out over the sea before her. "I'm relaxing in the sun. Fat and sassy. What are you doing?" she asked him in return.

He chuckled. "That's you. Fat and sassy. I have to get that in now, because after that baby pops out, you're going to go back down to your little size five frame and I won't be calling you fat anymore!" he laughed then. "I'm standing in the ice cream shop down the block from your place and I'm trying to decide what to bring you, but I can't make up my mind about what you want. So, help your brother out. What do you want?"

River Lea laughed at him. "You are too sweet for words, do you know that?" She shook her head slowly. "What did I ever do to deserve you?" She thought for a moment. "How about strawberry and lime, please?"

"You got it, sugar. I'll be over in a few," Gibby said with a grin she could hear through the phone. "And I'm lucky to have you too, River." He laughed a little and ended the call.

She set the phone down and smiled wide, looking out at the beach and the people who were strewn over it families with children, couples here and there, an old man with a metal detector walking slowly over an area of sand, kids at a tide pool poking at washed up sea creatures, and a few people playing volleyball. She grinned to herself.

It wasn't always the same scene, but it was often similar, and it always made her heart happy to look at it. People communing with each other and with nature, having fun, soaking up the sun, the sea, the sand, the saltwater, and each other. She didn't think life could get much better.

Gibby walked onto the deck with two big bowls of ice cream and a wide grin a few minutes later, and he handed one bowl to her and then sat on the chaise lounge on the other side of the table between them.

"Thank you so much, Gibby. This looks amazing. It's perfect!" She eyed it happily as she picked up the spoon.

"Of course! We have to spoil you and that little girl you're packing around. It's a hot day, you're like… what… twenty months pregnant. Ice cream is imperative. I had to. It's my duty as your best friend." He took a bite out of his rainbow sherbet and slowly slid the spoon out of his mouth as he gazed over the beach.

"So what are we looking at? Are there any hot guys I missed? Anyone I didn't see yet?" He scanned the beach goers carefully.

River Lea gave him a sidelong smirk and a wink. "You're always looking. Think you'll find true love in the sand and surf? Maybe… maybe someday you will. Today it's not looking too good. There are a few volleyball players, but none that are your type, and they all have girls with them. There's the beachcomber over there with the metal detector, but he's not likely to be a fun sugar daddy for you."

He sighed forlornly. "Someday my prince will come. I just know it. In the meantime, it's fun to hope, right?" He leaned back and took another bite. "It's too bad you never look."

She scoffed and rolled her eyes. "Ha! What am I going to do, waddle over to some hot guy and tell him, 'oh don't mind me, this kid will be out and gone in a few weeks and then we could see about dating'? Right. Also, you know I'm focused on other things. Much more important things."

Gibby looked over at her and cocked his brow slightly, "Yeah, but you could look. Looking is really nice."

"Looking leads to other things. Watching is fine, and eating ice cream with you is fine, but not looking. No thank you," she said resolutely as she jammed her spoon down into frozen pink and green mounds of ice cream.

They had just about cleaned out their bowls and were talking about everything under the sun when her phone rang and she looked over at the screen and frowned at the number that lit it up. "That's… so weird," she said quietly.

"What?" Gibby asked with his own frown. "Who's that?"

She picked it up and confusion shadowed her face. "I think it's the baby's mom and dad. I'm not supposed to hear from them until I go into labor. The clinic gives them all the updates on everything, and I haven't heard from them during this entire pregnancy."

She slid her finger over the screen and held the phone to her ear. "Hello?" she asked almost quizzically.

"River Lea?" the voice at the other end of the phone was male.

"Yes?" she asked, wondering about the call.

"Hi, I'm sorry to bother you. This is Matthew Chase. I hope I'm not catching you at a bad time." His voice was strained.

"Hi Matthew, what can I do for you?" River Lea looked over at Gibby and they shared a curious gaze.

He sighed heavily before he answered her. "I need to talk with you, as soon as possible. There are some… developments… on my end. I can send a car for you as soon as you are able to come meet me."

Her eyes widened and she tightened her fingertips slightly around the phone. "Uh… sure. I guess I'm free anytime."

"Would it work to have the car pick you up this evening? I can meet you for dinner and we can talk," he offered with a serious tone in his voice.

She shrugged as she replied. "Yeah, I guess that would be fine. Would six work?"

"Six o'clock is good. I'll send the car for you then. Thank you, I appreciate it," he answered, and then he said goodbye and ended the call. She set the phone back down on the table slowly and turned to look at Gibby with a confounded expression on her face.

"Well? What was that all about?" he asked interestedly.

River Lea blinked and gave her head a little shake. "Honestly? I don't know. It was the baby's father. He said there were 'developments' on his end," she curled her fingers in an air quote, "and he needs to talk to me right away. He's having me meet him for dinner tonight."

Gibby frowned. "Developments? What developments?"

She shook her head, lifting her hands in the air. "I have no idea. He didn't say. I can't guess. From the sound of his voice though, I'm not sure it sounds good, but I don't know him, so I guess we'll see."

"You better call me the minute you get home." Gibby looked at her seriously.

Waving her hand in the air, she laughed a little. "Of course! I'll let you know as soon as I can."

He gave her a nod of approval and they began to talk of other things. He stayed with her a long while, visiting and talking before he left her so that she could get ready to meet with the father of the baby she was carrying.

At five-thirty that night, a car pulled up to the house and the driver met River Lea at the door of her home and helped her into the back seat of the limo. She buckled herself in and looked around as the car drove away from her home and headed toward Silicon Valley where the parents of the baby she was carrying lived.

The driver pulled up to a refined-looking restaurant and helped River Lea out of the car. He told her that Mr. Chase would be waiting for her just inside the restaurant. She thanked him and went into the restaurant, finding Matthew Chase standing off to the side of the foyer, waiting for her.

He smiled at her and shook her hand. "How are you doing this evening?" he asked in a pleasant tone.

He was wearing a navy blue suit and he looked as if he could have just stepped off of the cover of a men's fashion magazine. She looked into his eyes to see if she could determine what might be going on with him, but his gaze seemed protected, and she couldn't discern anything.

"I'm doing really well, thank you," she answered him with a pleasant tone and greeting.

He waved to the manager of the restaurant who had been waiting on them, and they were taken to their table. It was a booth in quiet and secluded area of the room, set a little further aside from the rest of the dining area, offering some privacy to its occupants.

The subtle hum of conversation, the occasional clink of silverware against dishes, and soft music playing in the background filled in the silence between them as they sat. The manager took their drink orders and left them with menus.

River Lea looked around the restaurant. It was an establishment finer than any she had ever been in before. A cursory glance over the menu showed her a selection of entrees that she had never even imagined. She flicked her eyes up over the top of the menu momentarily to look at Matthew, wondering what he was going to order, and she saw that he had already set his menu down.

She decided on a pasta dish and slid her menu to the edge of the table. The waiter appeared out of nowhere, made a mental note of their order, and vanished once more. It felt surreal to River Lea, and she subconsciously ran her hands over the swell of her belly, soothing herself as well as the baby.

Matthew cleared his throat and looked at her, his brown eyes serious as he took her in. "I want to thank you for meeting me on such short notice. I know you weren't expecting this at all, and I appreciate you taking the time to meet with me."

"Well," she said in a soft voice, "it sounded like it was important. I'm glad to meet with you." She hesitated and looked around them for a moment before returning her gaze to him. "Amil won't be joining us?"

He pursed his lips and shook his head slowly, just once. "No, she won't. Actually, that's a big part of the reason why you and I are meeting tonight." He paused and lifted his drink, taking a long pull of it before setting it back on the table.

"Before I get into any of that though, I do want to be sure that you and the baby are both doing all right. The reports that we've gotten from the clinic show her to be a healthy little one, and I've been relieved to hear that. How are you getting along? Is there anything that you need?" he asked, eyes widening slightly as if he were encouraging her to let him know of any need that she might have.

She shook her head. "No, we're fine. I'm doing really well. I'm looking forward to the birth, you know, it'll be over then. You'll have your daughter, I'll get back to school. Life can get back to normal for us, but in the meantime, things are going really well. I'm happy."

He drew in a long, slow breath and dropped his gaze to the glass of brandy in front of him. Swirling the glass a moment, sending the amber liquid in waves around the inner circle of it, he pressed his lips together tightly and then raised his eyes again to meet River Lea's.

"I'm glad to hear that things are going well for you and the baby. That's at least some good news." He lifted one hand to his head and raked his fingers through his hair. "Things on my end aren't really going so well, though, and we need to talk about that."

River Lea watched him silently and waited, the very end of her nerves beginning to tingle slightly and it seemed as if all of the noise in the room that she had been hearing suddenly faded away, and everything in her was concentrated on the man sitting opposite her.

"There has been a change… a drastic change… in my life. Amil and I are no longer together, and there is no chance at all that we will ever be together at any time in the future." He sighed, letting out the full weight of the heavy air in his lungs.

"She's gone. I'm remaining at my home, and now with this child coming, I've had to give some serious thought as to what options are available to me." He furrowed his brow some as he held River Lea's steady gaze.

"I have given it considerable thought, and I just don't think I'm capable of raising a daughter on my own. I'm not really cut out for that." He looked down and she saw shame shadow his face as he took another long drink from his glass.

Her heart began to beat swiftly in her chest and she could hear the blood pounding in her ears. The words he'd said ricocheted through her mind as she tried to take them in and understand them. He wasn't with his wife any longer and he didn't think he could raise a daughter on his own. The daughter that was at that moment moving around inside of her, nudging her inner belly gently. She rubbed her fingers over the spot where the baby was pressing against her and she stared at Matthew. She still couldn't quite make out what it was he was trying to tell her.

"What are you saying to me?" she asked in a quiet voice, her eyes locked on him.

Matthew sighed again. "I can't... I don't think I can raise the baby on my own. I'm sorry; this is the last thing I would have ever thought might happen, but, I just don't feel like it would be the best situation for the child. I have another solution, though, and I want to propose that to you."

She stared at him, waiting to hear what he would say, astounded at what he had already told her. Everything in her had frozen as he had told her that he didn't think he could take the child. A moment later, everything in her was rushing like a wild river, crashing and coursing through her, and while everything about her demeanor and expression was still and pensive, everything just beneath the surface of her was in absolute chaos.

He looked back at her intently, and explained. "I'm going to make you a generous monetary offer if you are willing to keep the baby and raise it as your own. We can discuss the amount, but you wouldn't need to pay for anything or incur any expenses; I would make sure that you had more than enough to take care of everything." He paused a moment. "I just can't do it myself."

All the chaos that had been swirling wildly in her suddenly felt like it had culminated in her stomach and had come to a head. It built up almost immediately in her and it was almost as if an explosion was going off in her.

Her eyes grew wide and she gritted her teeth. "You want me to raise this baby for you? You hired me to be a surrogate mother, to carry your child, and now that it isn't convenient for you to raise your own baby, you're going to try to pay me off and foist it on me to raise? Are you serious?"

His face reddened and he looked down at the table shamefully before he looked back up at her. "Listen, I know it sounds really awful, but there's just no way that I could raise a child on my own! She doesn't want the baby anymore. She's doing… other things… and I'm just not in a position to try to be a single father. It would be completely unfair to the baby if I tried to do that. I can't do that to the child, and it just seems like you're the next best option. You won't have any financial hardship at all. I will take care of every expense."

He looked at her with pleading eyes and she could only feel anger burning away at her from inside. She gave her head a slow shake and glared hotly at him. "How dare you! If I could do it, you could do it, and this is *your child* for God's sake! You have a responsibility and a duty to her, above all else in your life! I'm in even less of a position to take care of her than you are! I only did this surrogacy as a way to pay for college! Being pregnant in college for a few short months is one thing, but being a single mother in college is something else entirely, and I'm not about to try to do it! This is not my responsibility, and your problems are not mine, so don't you even think about dragging me into them!"

Matthew looked at her imploringly, "Please! River Lea, I can't do it! I need you to consider this! There's no way that I could care for that little girl on my own! I have a company to run, I have countless other obligations that I have to take care of. I can't take her anymore! Not on my own!"

River Lea leveled her eyes at him. "This is your daughter, and you are going to take her home from the hospital when I give birth to her, and that is that! This isn't a business deal that you can just back out of! This is your child! I'm not about to change my whole life on a dime just because your marriage didn't work out!

I'm going back to school right after this baby is born. I have been working hard to get an education, to get my degree, and I'm going to keep working toward that. I'm not about to change all of that because your life isn't going the way that you thought it was going to go! You're a father now! Be one! You wanted this little girl enough to bring her to life and have me carry her, and now you're going to just walk away from her before she even sees the first day of her life?

That's not an option for you! She's your baby, you take her, and you raise her! I'm not about to take any amount of money to raise a child that isn't mine! I said I'd carry her and I am and that's all I'm doing. The rest is up to you."

She pushed herself up from the table and gave him one last hard look before turning to leave. He called out after her, and the other patrons in the restaurant looked up from their conversations and meals at the sudden volume of his voice.

"River Lea! Please!" He stood up to come after her and stopped short as she headed out of the door. She stood outside of the restaurant, her body trembling with anger, her breath short as she tried to calm herself down and gather her thoughts.

The driver who had brought her to the restaurant saw her from his parking space and pulled the car up to the door. He helped her into the back seat of the car and drove away. She stared out of the window, shock still registering through her, and tried to blink back the tears that stung her eyes.

By the time she walked in the front door of her home, she was no less angry than she had been when she left the restaurant. Pacing through her living room a few times, she finally reached for her cell phone and sat down to call Gibby, tapping her fingers on the table beside her as the phone on the other end of the line rang.

He answered it after the second ring. "Wow... that was fast. I thought you'd still be having dinner! So, what happened?" he asked curiously.

"You're not going to believe me when I tell you," she grumbled into the phone.

"Uh oh," he intoned with foreboding. "What did he want?"

"It isn't what he wants. It's what he doesn't want. He doesn't want his baby." She tried not to sound snappy when she spoke.

There was silence at the other end of the line for a long moment and the tone in Gibby's voice grew dark. "What do you mean he doesn't want the baby?"

River Lea sighed and leaned back into the sofa she was sitting on, covering her eyes with her hand.

"He said that he and his wife are not together anymore, and that she doesn't want the baby, and he can't raise it on his own, so he wanted me to take it and he was going to pay me some huge amount of money to keep it and raise it."

"What? He wants you to keep the baby and raise it?" Gibby almost shouted.

"That's what he said. I told him it's his kid and he has no business trying to get rid of it. I told him that I am in school, that I have my education in front of me right now and then my career after that, and that I'm not about to take his baby, no matter how much money he tries to buy me off with, and raise it. I told him he needs to raise his own baby, but he doesn't think he can do it as a single father," she ranted hotly as the memory of their conversation played out in her mind again.

Gibby was mumbling things in a low tone that she couldn't quite make out, but she was certain they weren't good. He finally spoke again. "So is he planning on taking that baby home from the hospital or is he just going to leave her with you?

How could he do that? It's his own baby! What kind of a jerk ditches his own baby that he paid for before it's even born?"

River Lea shook her head. "I don't know. All I do know is that I'm not keeping this baby. I have school coming up, and this is not my problem, it's his!"

Gibby swore under his breath a few more times and sighed. "Okay, hang on. Hang on. Let's think about this. You have a contract with him. Right? Didn't the clinic have all of you sign a contract?"

"Yes…" she replied quietly, opening her eyes and lowering her hand. The clinic had them sign an enormous stack of papers. She hadn't thought about it at all during her conversation, but when Gibby brought it up, she could start to see some logic and some light at the end of the tunnel. Matthew would have to take the baby.

"So that's one aspect of it," Gibby said thoughtfully. "You have the contract. That doesn't help him much, though. So let's look at what he offered you. Did he tell you how much money he was willing to give you?"

"Gibby!" she chided him.

"No, seriously, I know it's not what you were thinking, but let's look at everything. We said you have the contract and that is one road that could be taken. This is just another road. Now, how much money did he offer you?" he asked in a calm tone.

She rolled her eyes. "He didn't say. He just said he would take care of everything and that I would have no expense. I wouldn't let him get to the part about money. He's a billionaire, though, so I can't imagine it would be some small amount."

"Okay, okay. That's something to work with." He continued, "So, let's say that you did take him up on his offer and you took a huge lump sum settlement and you kept the baby. So, you'd have money to raise the baby with, and to pay for daycare and all of that, your education would be completely paid for. You probably wouldn't have to worry about finances for the rest of your life, or at least until the baby turns eighteen. I know that's not what you have in mind, but it is an option to consider."

"I can't consider that," she replied sternly.

"I know you have other plans. I know it. So, let's think about what else we could do with this situation. Let's get creative. Why doesn't the mother want the baby? What mother doesn't want her own baby?" he asked in amazement.

Sighing, River Lea shook her head. "I have no idea. Some mothers just aren't cut out to be mothers and they don't want their babies. I don't know if it's actually true though, she wasn't there. She didn't tell me that she didn't want it; he told me that she didn't want it. So, you're right about looking at other possibilities. I could try to contact her and make sure she doesn't want it instead of just taking his word for it."

"Right?" Gibby asked, his tone lightening somewhat. "So, that's another option. Let's take a look at Dad and figure that out. Why doesn't he want this baby?"

Frowning, she knit her brow and thought about it carefully. "Well, he said he has a business to take care of and he doesn't think he could raise her on his own. He doesn't know how to be a single father. He seemed really sad about it, like he had wanted her so much before, but now he just seems afraid, sort of in a panic, like he has no idea what to do. I think his wife must have left him and he's in a really low place. Kind of lost."

"Well that's no good. I wonder…" Gibby paused a moment and she knew he was thinking deeply. "I wonder if he thinks the baby will be a reminder of her and that might be too difficult for him to see every day. He hasn't really bonded with the baby, because he hasn't been around you and been able to feel the excitement of her growing and changing all the time in you. He's missed out on all of that. As far as he is concerned, there is no emotional attachment for him yet. So, what if we work on changing that?" he sounded as if he had happened upon a brilliant idea.

"What do you mean?" River Lea asked curiously.

"What if he developed an emotional attachment to the baby before she's born?" He answered her question with his own question.

River Lea frowned. "Gibby, what are you talking about?"

"Hear me out… just hear me out a minute here…." He paused and took a breath. "He doesn't have an emotional attachment to the baby because he hasn't been around it. Now it's possible that he doesn't want it because it might remind him of his wife that left him.

Now he's afraid that he can't raise it on his own. So you need to find a way to connect him to that baby before the baby is born, so he will want to take it home. Help him bond with her so that he wants to be there when she is born, and wants to be there to take her home and raise her. Then you're off the hook and she's with her dad, and everything is the way that it should be."

"That's…" she began to say, but then she began to think about what he had suggested and the idea of it began to stick in her mind. "Gib… that's brilliant! That's… that might just work! Except for one thing."

"What thing?" he asked doubtfully.

"How am I supposed to get him to bond with this baby? I don't see him," she replied with a note of dejection.

"You have maternity appointments at the doctor every week now, don't you? For your last month… right?" He sounded hopeful.

"Yes, I do," River Lea answered, a small smile tugging at the corner of her lips.

"Well, invite him to come to the appointments with you. Make sure he's there for every one of them. He'll hear the baby's heartbeat, maybe get a sonogram and he can see her on the monitor… help him connect to her so that he wants her. It has to work. What do you think?" Gibby sounded enormously pleased with himself.

"I think that's a brilliant idea and I love it. I'll call him in the morning and tell him that I will consider his offer if he goes with me to the appointments." She smiled widely. "I also think that I have one of the best friends ever. Thank you, Gibby. I love you."

"You're welcome, River. I love you too. Let me know how it goes." He bade her goodnight, and she ended the call and let her head fall back against the sofa, closing her eyes with a sigh of relief. It was going to be simple. Help Matthew fall in love with his daughter, and he would take her home. She would be free to go to school, and the deal would be done just like it should have been to begin with. River Lea thought again how lucky she was to have Gibby, and how fortunate it was that he was so clever.

She looked down at her swollen belly and smiled, rubbing her hand over it. "Don't you worry, Charlie. I'm going to help you. I'm going to make sure that your dad falls in love with you before you ever take your first breath, and he's going to be so excited to take you home. You'll see. You will be the more important person in his life." The baby pushed and nudged against her hand.

Chapter 2

River Lea picked up the phone the next morning and called Matthew Chase. Her hands trembled slightly as she dialed, and she felt as if her heart was in her throat when the other line began to ring.

He answered with a hopeful sounding hello. "This is Matthew."

Taking a deep breath and swallowing hard, she spoke. "Hi Matthew. This is River Lea. I know I left abruptly yesterday, and I'm sorry for that. You really caught me off guard with your… request." She curled her fingers more tightly around the telephone.

She heard a sigh escape him. "I realize that it was probably quite a shock for you, and I'm sorry about that. I know it's a lot to take in and consider, and I know it's a lot for me to ask."

"Well, it is a lot to consider, and that's something that I wanted to talk with you about," she replied as pleasantly as she could. "After I got home last night, I was thinking that it might be good for you to come along with me to one of her appointments. I have one tomorrow afternoon. We could talk about your offer."

River Lea didn't want to make any promises, or make it seem like she was accepting his offer, but she did want to get him to go to the doctor's appointment with her, and she guessed that telling him that they could talk about his offer was probably the best way to do that.

There was a momentary silence at his end of the line before he spoke. He sounded uncertain. "We could talk about it over the phone, or meet again for coffee or something. I feel like that might be a better idea. I don't know that going to one of the obstetrician appointments would be the best choice for me."

She frowned in frustration with his hesitation. "Well, I think it's only fair. I'm carrying your child, and you're talking about leaving her with me. I think you could sacrifice twenty minutes at the doctor's office with me so that we can talk about what our options are."

Matthew sighed again and relented. "All right. I guess that doesn't really seem like much to ask on your side. I can do that. Where should I meet you?"

Relief flooded her and she closed her eyes and smiled before opening them as she answered him. "You could come by the house and pick me up at two. We'll just go together from here. Would that be all right?"

"Yes, that would be fine. I'll see you then," he replied. "River Lea... thank you for calling me back."

"You're welcome," she answered with no small amount of satisfaction. When she ended the call, she tried not to feel too accomplished, because she knew she had a long way to go in convincing Matthew that he needed to take his baby girl when she was born, but it was at least one step in the right direction, and that was something to be thankful for.

He came when he said he would the next day, and she greeted him with a smile at the door, reminding herself that if she was going to be successful in her mission, she was going to have to be friendly with him and get him to want to spend time with her, and she knew that arguing with him as she had when they were at dinner wasn't going to be the way to do that.

He blinked as he looked at her, his eyes sweeping over her once as he took her in. "You look beautiful…" he seemed to stumble through his spoken thought, "…radiant, I guess."

She smiled in surprise and ran her hand over the soft yellow sundress she was wearing. She liked the way that it made her mocha skin seem to glow, and her blue eyes stand out a little more. "Thank you," she answered him sweetly.

His brown eyes flickered to her enormous belly as she stood there before him. "How are you feeling?" he asked, a pained expression shadowing his face for a moment.

Without a thought to her reaction, she placed her hand on her stomach and rubbed gently. "We're both doing fine, thank you." She picked up her bag and closed her front door behind her. He turned and walked with her to his car and she glanced over at him with a little surprise.

She had only seen him twice; once at the initial appointment at the clinic and once at their dinner meeting. Both times she'd seen him, he had been wearing a suit. She was surprised to see him dressed in a polo shirt and cotton pants. The polo shirt hugged his upper physique, hinting at the solid cut of muscle beneath it. When she realized she was looking at him, she turned her head away swiftly and blinked, chastising herself mentally for letting herself do anything of the kind.

He helped her into the car and she gave him directions to the doctor's office. It was quiet for a few minutes before he spoke, and when he did, he began with small talk; things about the home she lived in and what she did for fun. It was the beginning of getting to know her, and she knew that, but at every chance she could, she interjected information about the pregnancy and the baby, filling Matthew in on all of the experiences and changes that he had missed over the course of it all.

He sat in the waiting room with her, looking around nervously at the photographs of new babies on the wall, and the child's play center in the corner. She watched him from the corner of her eye as he leaned forward and flipped through the parenting magazines on the small table before them, touching them briefly before he pulled his hand back empty, and looked around before turning his gaze to her.

"So, how do these appointments work? What is the doctor looking for?" he asked with no small amount of uncertainty.

She smiled at him. "Well, I'm coming once a week now for the last month. The doctor is checking everything for both the baby and me, to be sure it's all going as it should, so that we have an easier and on time delivery."

"Every week?" he asked in surprise. She nodded and he gave her a nod in return as he grew thoughtful. "You said everything is okay, though... right? Everything is going along as it should?"

River Lea nodded. "It is. She's healthy and strong, and developing just as she should be."

He was quiet a moment and was about to reply when the nurse called them back to the examination room. Matthew stood and watched silently as the doctor measured her belly and then rubbed gel over it and positioned the sonogram tool on it.

The lights in the room were dimmed and a monitor lit up, showing the baby as she rested curled up in her fetal position inside of River Lea. River Lea didn't watch the screen. Her eyes were on Matthew.

He stared at first, his mouth open slightly as images of his daughter appeared before him for the first time. It looked to River Lea like he couldn't believe his own eyes, and in that moment she knew that taking him to the doctor's appointments was exactly the right thing to do. Gibby had been right. She glanced at the monitor herself a couple of times, but the rest of time her eyes were on Matthew.

He began to ask the doctor questions about her, just a few at first, and then more as his curiosity got the better of him. He turned his head to River Lea and asked, "What's that sound?" It was a repetitive gushing sound, like a pulse moving through water.

River Lea laughed a little. "That's Charlie's heartbeat!" she told him as he gaped at the monitor.

He blinked a few times and looked back down at her. "...Charlie?"

"Oh… well… I sort of started calling her Charlotte; I like that name, but I call her Charlie as a nickname," she explained gently. "I hope that doesn't bother you that I came up with a name. It's just temporary. Did you have a name picked out?" she asked, leading him to talk about his daughter again, and involve him in any way that she could.

He shook his head slowly as he watched the imagery of the baby moving and kicking. "No… we didn't really get that far." His voice was quiet and a sadness showed in his eyes.

River Lea bit her lower lip and realized that she might have pushed him a little too far. She didn't want to open up wounds; she was trying to get him interested, not scare him away. "Would you like to feel her move?" she asked.

He looked for a moment like he might say yes; his eyes steady on her rounded belly, but then he began to shake his head. "No, I don't think so," he answered. She could see that he meant it, and she made up her mind right then that she was going to get him to come to the next baby appointment and try to get him to feel the baby move then. She had some time to work on him, and she decided that she was going to do everything that she could to help him bond with his daughter.

He looked as if he was trying to change the subject when he spoke again, his eyes meeting hers. "So… Charlotte. I like that name. Why did you decide to call her Charlotte?" There was a hint of interest in his voice.

She smiled and touched her fingertips to the bare skin on her belly, rubbing them gently over the rounded mass there. "Well, that was my grandmother's name. I loved her; she was sassy and smart, and she really made an amazing life for herself, even though there were hardships along the way. I'd like to think that her spirit could live on in other young girls, and when I found out that Charlie was a girl, I decided to call her Charlotte after my grandmother because this baby has got a lot of spunk and attitude. She's a busy little thing in there. Sometimes I wonder if she's going to be patient enough to wait the whole term before she comes out into the world to take it over!"

River Lea laughed at the idea, knowing she was probably right about the little one in her, and Matthew laughed with her. The tension between them eased and she felt it change and shift, and it became friendly, as if somehow they were comrades of a sort, on the same team, and that was a big relief to her. It made the possibility of sending Matthew home with his daughter when she was born, a little more realistic.

When the appointment was over, he helped her into the car and began to drive back toward her home. She turned to him as the city passed by them, and eyed him carefully. "So, what did you think of the appointment?" She was curious and she wanted to keep his mind focused on Charlie.

He was quiet a long moment and she thought she saw a bit of confliction cross his face as he answered her. "It was… kind of unreal. I never expected to see the baby before… to see her before she was born. I didn't know what it would be like.

It was…" he paused a moment, seeming to search for the right word, "…incredible."

She felt hope and relief course through her and she let a long sigh out slowly, hoping that she was closer to her goals. He changed the subject then, furrowing his brow slightly and raising the volume of his voice.

"So, are you hungry at all? Could I interest you in something to eat?" he asked, glancing over at her with an expression bordering on seriousness. She knew then that he was done talking about the baby.

Giving it a little thought, she nodded. "Yes, actually. I am a bit hungry. There's a little café not far from my house. We could go there. They make great sandwiches."

He nodded and his shoulders dropped some as he relaxed a bit. "That sounds perfect." She gave him directions, and a short while later they were collecting their sandwiches and strolling down the beach slowly, late lunch in hand.

"So, what are you in school for?" he asked, peeling the paper from his sandwich.

She swallowed the bite she was chewing and smiled. "I'm in school to be a marine biologist. I just love the ocean and all of the life in it. It feels like home to me. I want to be able to work to clean it up and protect it. There's still so much that we don't know about it. It is a vital dynamic of our planet and something that basically every species needs to survive; at least in one way or another. I want to spend my life taking care of it. It's a labor of love."

He stopped walking, pausing in place with his sandwich in his hand halfway to his mouth, looking at her with some surprise. "Really? Wow... that's wonderful! I invest in start-up companies, and two of the ones I've just invested in within the last two months are focused on ocean clean up and sustainability and biodiversity. I was really interested in everything that they presented to me when I interviewed them for funding possibilities, and I wound up doing more research than they initially came to me with. That's so… interesting… that you're into doing that kind of work as well. I like that."

He gave her a grin and then brought his sandwich to his mouth for the bite he'd halted partway. It was River Lea's turn to look at him in surprise. "Really? You're helping to make ecological changes that way? That's fantastic!" She was more than thrilled to hear it. As they walked along further, she thought about what he had told her, feeling even more glad that she was taking the time to try to get him interested in his daughter, because when she did get him to take his daughter home, the girl would be raised by an environmentally concerned parent. Happiness radiated in her.

She decided to try another way to connect him with Charlie. "I was thinking about what you were saying about you raising the baby on your own, and I understand that trying to do that would be pretty challenging, but I wondered if perhaps maybe getting a full time nanny for the baby might work out for you. You know, someone to take care of her most of the time while you're working or busy, and then that would take a lot of the stress off you. You could still have her, and share the responsibility and work. Have you given any thought to a situation like that?"

River Lea looked at him with an encouraging smile, hoping with everything in her that he was willing to listen to her and consider taking his daughter home with him, because there were other solutions besides giving her up.

He shrugged and shook his head. "I don't know... I guess I haven't really thought about that. I didn't think about other options when Amil left... I just knew I couldn't bring the baby home and do it on my own. I never thought about a nanny."

"Well, now you're thinking of it. There are great nannies out there; find a live-in nanny and you're problem is solved." River Lea continued to speak positively to him. Charlie turned in her and nudged her with her foot a couple of times. River Lea's hand went to the top side of her stomach, rubbing gently where the baby had kicked her, and in her mind she told the baby that she was working on talking her daddy into taking her home.

Matthew sighed and raked his free hand through his hair, frowning. "I don't know. I'm not sure that would work. Right now I really think the best plan would be for you to keep the baby, and for me to take care of all of the costs."

River Lea frowned then, and furrowed her brow. She could see that she wasn't making any headway with her bright idea of a nanny. She remained quiet for a few minutes as they walked together in silence, eating their sandwiches and thinking. The ocean rolled in beside them, churning and splashing, hushing the shore, and the repetition of the waves soothed the frustration in her.

She considered another tactic. "Well, I'm not sure what's going on with you and your wife, except for what you've shared with me, that she left you, and that the two of you won't be getting back together, but… what if you found someone else and fell in love again? I realize it might not seem like it could be a possibility now, but it might be in your future. You never know. You're a smart, successful, good-looking guy. You have a lot to offer a lady. It seems fair to bet that you'll find someone in the future and settle down again. What if you had a nanny to begin with, and then someday when you fall in love, you could create a new family then?"

It was a long shot, but by that point she was willing to do whatever she could to convince him that Charlotte should go home with him. She looked over at him as she spoke, and his reaction took her a little by surprise.

She heard his breath catch and he gave his head a slight shake as his eyes narrowed and he looked away from her. The smile that had been spread on his face vanished, and in his hesitation, she saw something between regret and pain shadow his face.

He didn't answer her for a long moment, and she almost spoke again, just to break the silence, but just as she was wondering how to change what had been said, he found his place and voiced his thoughts.

"I don't know that I could love again. That seems like a million light years away from where I am right now. I was with her for five years; we thought it was going to last forever at the beginning, but then it began to cool off and it got cold between us a couple of years ago." He tossed the paper wrapper from his eaten sandwich into a trash bin and then pushed his hands down into the pockets of his pants as he continued to talk with River Lea.

"I wanted to try to save the marriage; divorce was the last thing on my mind, but there was just… no spark, no love… nothing left. I was desperate to make it work with her, rather than giving up on it. I'm not normally a quitter. That's one of the reasons I've been so successful." He sighed and stared down at the sand before him as he walked, looking as if the world around him had somehow suddenly shrunk to just the two of them and nothing else existed.

"I told her that I thought we ought to have a baby. I felt that if we started a family, we might be able to find some purpose to be together, and I hoped that we could both fall in love with the child, and that it would ignite the spark between us once again. She agreed to try, and we did try for a little while, though not as much as I had hoped we would.

She just…" he pressed his lips together in a tight line and then exhaled slowly, "…she just couldn't get pregnant, and so I told her we'd find a surrogate to carry the baby for us. She seemed to readily accept that idea, and we went to the clinic with our plan and found you."

River Lea thought back to the day she'd met the couple. It was a one-time meeting, and she recalled how she had thought of Amil as cool and aloof. She frowned and the new insight into the woman she had met somehow made the other woman's manner easier to understand.

"We thought it would work, but… I guess there was just no saving the marriage." He stopped short of his explanation then and a troubled look darkened his eyes. He said no more for a while, and River Lea knew that silence was the best thing for them just then.

They came to a place where the beach turned into rocks and boulders, and they turned around and headed back to the café. She took a deep breath and crossed her arms in front of her chest, speaking with more tenderness than she had up to that point.

"I'm so sorry that things turned out the way that they did for you. That's really awful." She paused a moment and looked up at him. "Think of the baby, though. Think of how much joy and happiness she will bring you. Think of all the real honest, true love and fulfillment that you would find with her. That's so much better than what you lost, or even a possible future love with a woman; a bond with a child is a lifelong relationship, and one that is better than any other relationship that you might ever have again.

Don't you feel that you owe it to her and to yourself to give that love and that relationship a chance? She could heal all of the pain that you're feeling from the loss of your marriage." River Lea firmly believed every word she was saying, and there was a passionate conviction in her tone that he didn't miss, but she saw that her words did not breach his wall, even before he spoke again.

"I really don't think I'm emotionally ready for the responsibilities of raising a baby, and I know I'm not at all prepared for the challenge of single fatherhood, whether there is a nanny around or not. It's just not going to be right for me to do this." He exhaled heavily and then looked into River Lea's ocean-blue eyes.

"Look, I can really appreciate what you're trying to do here, but I truly do believe that the best thing for her and for me is for you to keep her and let me just take care of every and any expense that you two might have for the next few decades. I'm glad to pay for everything, and I'll sign her right over to you, but… I just know that I am not ready for her, and I don't think I ever will be.

I can see that you are a woman of morals and strength; you are intelligent, kind, and thoughtful, and I feel like the best way for me to handle this, is just to have you keep her. It would be best for me, and what's more, it would be best for her. Please… River Lea, please just consider it. Give it some honest thought." He pleaded with her, and more than anything she could see the pain and doubt in his eyes.

She wondered, as she watched him, if she would be able to get past that wall of uncertainty before Charlotte was born. She knew she was going to try with everything in her. She had promised the baby, and she was a woman of her word.

River Lea tilted her head thoughtfully and bit her lower lip. Then, she raised one eyebrow and spoke with a gentle but slightly challenging tone. "I'll tell you what. I'll consider your offer if you come to next week's appointment with me. I'll be honest; going this whole pregnancy alone has been challenging, and I'm a little nervous about giving birth to her. I've never given birth before, as you know, and I could really use the support. Will you come with me next week and help me through it... and then I will give some serious consideration to your request?"

She only said she'd consider it. She knew full well that she wasn't about to change her mind, but she wasn't promising to change her mind; she was promising to consider it, and thinking about it as much as she was could be called considering it.

He scrunched his face up a moment thinking about it, and then he nodded. "All right. I guess that isn't too much to ask at all. You're doing all of the work here. Yeah, no problem. I'll come with you next week. Just let me know when the appointment is, and I'll come pick you up again if that's all right."

River Lea grinned and nodded. It felt like they were play a game of real life chess, and she had just scored a major move that he wasn't quite aware of. "Yes, thank you! I'll give you a call about it."

They reached the café and got back into his car and he drove her home. She watched him leaving from the front window of her house, as she rubbed her hand over her belly.

"We'll get him, Charlie. Don't you fret baby girl, you just wait and see. We're going to make him fall in love with you and you'll be going home with daddy the day you come shining into this world. You just wait and see. I'm going to make it happen, and you do what you can to help me. Okay?" She looked down at the big round belly beneath her fingers.

Charlie gave River Lea's hand a couple of strong kicks, and River Lea laughed and smiled. "That's my girl."

Chapter Three

Morning sun shone brilliantly through the kitchen windows, illuminating her sunny yellow and white kitchen brightly, and making River Lea feel as warm as the glow looked. She carefully poured a cup of blueberries into the blender before her on the counter, and then added sliced strawberries and a half a cup of raspberries. She scooped in some yogurt and a small bit of honey and cinnamon, put the lid on the blender and pressed the button to churn it into a shake for her breakfast.

Charlie kicked at her and she laughed, looking down at her belly as she rubbed the hardened mound. "I'm working on it, kiddo. It's coming. I hope you learn some patience as you grow up!" She smiled as she took the lid off of the blender and poured her fruit smoothie into a glass.

Her cell phone rang and she reached for it, happy to see who it was that was calling her.

"Good morning Gibby. How are you doing?" Her smile grew a little wider.

He sounded as if he had been wide awake for a while, and she envied him that, stifling a little yawn as he greeted her. "Good morning to you! I'm good. I was out on a date with Brad last night, and it was a lot of fun. We went to a new restaurant and then a movie, and we really enjoyed ourselves."

"Nice! You've kind of been seeing a lot of him lately…" she teased him a little with her tone, and he gave a surrendering moan back to her.

"I have… he's really nice. I'm just enjoying his company for now. I guess we'll see how it all goes. How's the wee one today?" he shifted topics and she could hear the smile in his voice.

"Charlie's good. She's impatient for breakfast, though, so we're focusing on that right now," River Lea answered him with a soft and pleasant sigh.

He paused a moment. "Has anything new happened with her dad? How's that coming along?"

River Lea carried her smoothie in one hand and held the phone in her other hand against her ear as she walked out of the house onto her back deck and sat in the sunshine. "Well... I got him to come to the appointment with me, and that was good. I could see that it was a totally unexpected experience for him. I don't think he's seen any of her pictures or anything before the appointment. I think it was the very first time he ever laid eyes on her. He was really moved by it, and he was curious about it, but he kept his distance anyway."

"What do you mean he kept his distance?" Gibby sounded confused.

She pushed her lip out in a slight pout. "Well, he was in the exam room with me, you know, watching the monitor and listening to the doctor and all that, but I asked him if he wanted to feel her move and kick and he wouldn't do it. He was polite about it, but he still said no, and I knew then

70

that it would take some time to get him more comfortable with her. This making him fall in love with her plan of ours is going to take a little while. I just hope that it happens before she's born."

Gibby hummed thoughtfully. "Mmmm. Well… it's a step in the right direction at least, and that's further than he was when he asked you to take her. Has he changed his mind about that?"

River Lea sighed. "No. He took me to the doctor's appointment and brought me home, and we went for a walk and talked some. He's going through a hard time right now, and I can understand that, but I think he's connecting the baby too much to the negative stuff going on in his life, and I want to try to find a way to disassociate her with all of that, if I can."

"What bad stuff? It isn't anything that will affect Charlie, is it?" he asked apprehensively.

"Well," River looked up thoughtfully and ran her finger over her chin, "yes and no. I guess he and his wife were having some difficulties in their marriage and they thought that having a baby together might get things back on track, but then partway through the pregnancy she left him, and now he's faced with having to raise Charlie on his own. It scares him, I think, and I'm pretty sure that the baby reminds him too much of his wife. I tried to explain to him that the baby will make him happy and help him heal, but he just can't see that from where he is now. He's really struggling. I can see that he's a good guy, but he's just in a really rough spot. Tough to deal with."

Gibby was quiet a moment. "So, what do you think your next step will be?" he asked in a soft voice.

River Lea had been thinking of nothing but all of the steps she was going to take to make sure that she got Matthew to a point where he would be glad to take his daughter home. She had promised Charlie that it would happen, and she was hell bent to succeed.

"Well, we kind of connected some while we were doing the appointment and talking, so I think he looks at me as sort of a friend now, and that's good. I need to help him learn to trust me so that he values my opinion somewhat, at least. He did push again for me to take her and keep her, telling me that he was going to pay for everything, and I knew that I couldn't just tell him no.

I think if he winds up coming to another appointment, or all of the rest of the appointments, he will start to get more excited for her and he will feel closer to her, so I used his request as a means to get him back to the doctor's office." She bit her lip and grimaced slightly, knowing that Gibby might not think too much of her tactic.

"I told him that I would consider his offer if he came to another appointment with me, and he said yes. So, he is going to be at the doctor's next week." She almost felt like holding her breath, waiting to hear what Gibby thought of her move. She didn't have to wait long at all.

"You what? You can't do that! You have to get that baby girl into his arms and get him to take her home! You lied to him!" His tone was almost scolding.

She shook her head and sat up a little. "No, it wasn't a lie. I am considering it. Not... not like he wants me to. When I said I was considering it, what I meant was that I was just giving it a lot of thought. All the thought I can, on how to get out of his request and convince him to take her. So, in a way I'm considering it, just not the way he is hoping I will." She was quiet a moment and looked down.

"Do you think that's bad? Dishonest?"

She felt a little sorry, but not sorry enough not to have done it. "I have to do something. I can't just let it go. It was sort of a bargain between us. I said I would consider it if he came to the doctor appointment with me, and he agreed to that. So, we are both getting what we want out of it. Kind of."

Speaking it out loud to her best friend made it sound a little less upstanding than it had been in her mind. "I have to try. I have to do something. I promised Charlie that I would do anything that I could to get her dad to take her home!"

Gibby sighed. "You're not doing anything really wrong. Everything you're doing is for the greater good. That's important. Don't worry about it. The morality police are not going to come banging at your door, and I'm not disappointed in you, so don't feel bad.

You're on the right track. What you really have to focus on is getting him to fall for her, and one way to do that is to keep him around her, whether that means talking to you or going to the appointments, or whatever else you can think of. Just… do your best to make sure he's around you as much as he can be during these final weeks. You don't have much time left to make this miracle happen."

"Don't I know it?" she agreed wholeheartedly with him. "I'm doing all I can. Trust me." she thought of the appointment to come and knew that she would really have to put some effort into making sure that they spent more time together than just at the appointment.

She took a long sip of her smoothie and set the glass down, leaning back in her chair again as she looked out on the morning sunlight glittering off of the gently rolling surface of the sea. "So, what did you and Brad go see last night?" she asked curiously. The last thing she wanted to do was monopolize the conversation, though she did appreciate his dedication and support to her and the whole situation with the baby who was moving in her belly at that moment.

They talked for a while after that, and when they hung up the phone, he made her promise to keep him updated on everything that was happening with Matthew. She lifted her chin a little and took a deep breath of morning air into her lungs, at least as far as her eight-month maternity body would let her breath in, and she patted the baby bump.

"We're working on it, little girl. Don't you worry; it's going to happen. We're working on it," she said with a smile.

***

Matthew came as promised the following week, showing up on time to pick her up from her home. He looked happy when she opened the door, and she could tell that he was genuinely glad to see her. It made her feel the same about seeing him.

When she stepped outside her home, closing the door behind her, he gave her an amiable hug around the shoulders, and she hugged him in return, thinking how good it was that they were on friendly terms. She knew that it would be easier to convince him to take on his fatherly duties if they were getting along and sharing mutual respect and friendship.

He asked her about the baby and as she told him all of the sweet little things that she could think of—anything that might endear him to Charlie, he listened intently and asked questions, responding with interest as she answered. It was encouraging to her and it gave her hope.

He helped her out of the car and into the doctor's office, and as he did, he reached his hand to take hers in support, and he stood nearer to her as they walked, placing his hand upon her back or her shoulder occasionally. It felt like a comfort to her to feel his gentle touch, and she didn't shy away from it. They chatted easily in the waiting room; much more easily than they had the week before when he had gone to a previous visit with her there.

The nurse called them back to the examination room, and River Lea saw that he was much more comfortable with her and with the whole process the second time around. He seemed to her to look more eager as the monitor flickered to life and images of the baby appeared when the imaging tool moved over her belly.

It warmed her heart and gave her a powerful sense of relief as she saw him becoming more engaged with it. Matthew looked surprised at the growth and changes that the baby had gone through in a week. His curiosity showed in the conversation he had with the doctor in looking at the information on the images. River Lea said very little during the appointment, but instead just watched Matthew as little by little, he took a gradual interest in what was happening with his daughter.

When they left the facility, he helped her to the car and just as she was about to get in, she felt fully inspired to push him just a little further and baby Charlie seemed to want to help out as much as she could. Standing beside the door that he was holding open, River Lea looked up into Matthew's eyes and grinned.

"She's moving around a lot right now, would you like to feel her?" she asked with more than a hint of excitement.

He blinked at her and his mouth fell open just a little. "Would I… uh… I don't think—" he sounded to her as if he was going to say no again, and she felt compelled to try just a little harder.

"It's really okay. You should feel this! It's incredible! Here… give me your hand." She hadn't meant to interrupt him, but she didn't want him to get the "no" out of his mouth before she even had a chance to get him to the next step with his daughter.

Hesitating a minute, he finally let her take his hand and place it at the top of her belly. She laid his palm flat and he slowly spread his fingers a little, almost looking as if he had a grip on a basketball. Charlie did her part well, kicking and turning, nudging his hand firmly from within.

At the very first feel of her beneath his hand, Matthew's eyes opened wide and his breath caught. It was as if he had frozen from the hair down, and River Lea was delighted to see just how much the new connection with his daughter was affecting him.

He was still for a moment, and then a smile began to grow over his face, and the smile became a laugh as Charlie moved even more. They stood that way, with him holding his hand on River Lea's belly, for a little while, until Charlotte calmed down and stilled, and then he pulled his hand slowly from her belly and shook his head almost as if he was in a daze.

"That was amazing! I've never felt anything like that... I didn't expect..." he trailed off then, and River Lea saw the light and happiness in his eyes began to fade, like a thick dark cloud had suddenly moved over the sun, blocking everything in its shadow.

The smile left his face and he turned away from her, furrowing his brow as he pursed his lips together tightly and sighed. "We need to go. I have another commitment that I have to get to," he said shortly. His tone had grown cool, and River Lea wondered if she had gone too far with him.

Wordlessly, she sank into the car and he closed the door behind her. The drive home was quiet between them, and it worried her, washing away the hope and faith that she had found in the advancement she thought they had made that day. It felt like it was one step forward and two steps back with him.

Matthew dropped her off at her house, helping her to the door and turning to go abruptly, with a short goodbye and no hug of fond farewell or anything of the kind. She stood in her doorway, watching him get back into his car and leave, and as he disappeared down the road and around the corner, she moved her own hand over her belly, soothing the baby inside.

"I know that didn't go like we thought it would, but you did really well, baby girl. You connected with him, just like he needs you to, but it's going to take some more work. We'll get him, honey. Don't worry. I'm going to make sure that your daddy falls smack in love with you and wants nothing more in the world than to take you home with him." She frowned and told herself that if she expected Charlie to believe her, she better believe what she was saying herself.

She walked out to the back deck and watched as the afternoon sun bathed the beach and sea in golden light, and she called Gibby to tell him how it had gone. He heard the disappointment in her voice right away, and he was sympathetic to her situation.

"So… he just left you? Just took off?" His voice mirrored the dejection that she herself felt.

"Yeah, pretty much. He was great at the appointment, right up until I had him feel the baby move outside of the doctor's office, and he actually really seemed to love it at first, but then I think it kind of hit him that he was connecting with his own baby; a baby he was going to give up completely, and that was just too much for him.

I don't think he's even considered taking the baby home yet. I feel as though it was a connection with her that he hadn't expected and wasn't ready for, and it just got real for him, real fast, and it took him by surprise." She sighed and her shoulders slouched just a little.

Gibby was quiet on the other end of the line for a few moments and she knew he was thinking about what she had just told him. "River, I'm just going to say it like this. This man has talked himself clean out of having that child. As far as he is concerned, it's not going home with him and he isn't planning on it being with him ever, and then you go and little by little begin to make her a part of his life.

That's probably taking him for a little bit of a spin. I think you're right about him not being ready for that. I think it's going to take some time. I just hope that it doesn't take too much time. You're down to the wire on this."

Shaking her head, her eyes wide, she agreed wholeheartedly with him. "I know that and you're right. We're doing our best, Charlie and me. It has to work, though. Seriously. I feel bad for this kid, but I can't keep her. He has got to man up and do this thing, and I think he will, if I can get him to be just a little more involved."

"Is he going to next week's baby appointment?" Gibby asked hopefully.

"He didn't say. We didn't talk about anything after he felt her moving. He just drove me home and then he left and that was that." Frowning, she tipped her head thoughtfully. "I'll call him. I'll get him to come. Maybe he just needs a little time. I can try to make sure that he gets that. I want him interested for the next appointment, not scared, and he was more than a little interested this time. So, at least we're getting closer!" Her frown turned into a small smile and her voice lightened.

"I'll let you know what he says. Hopefully, it'll happen." She gave a nod.

"I'm crossing everything for you both." Her best friend replied in complete support.

They talked of other things for a while, and he finally said goodbye to her. Her thoughts stayed on Matthew all that afternoon and evening and she tried to come up with as many creative ways as she could to ensure that he would feel compelled to come to the next appointment, and perhaps even to spend more time than just that with her. She knew that the more he was around her and Charlie, the more he would connect, and the greater the chances were that he would do the right thing and take his daughter home.

River Lea waited a few days, and then she decided it was time to call him. She hoped that the nerves he'd felt would have settled by then, and he would be receptive to going back to the doctor's again. A surge of relief moved through her when he answered his phone fairly quickly. She breathed out a sigh and smiled with encouragement in her heart.

"Hi, Matthew, it's River Lea," she told him after he said hello.

His voice was friendly and that also bolstered her courage. "Well hello! How are things going? How are the two of you doing?"

"We're good. She's getting bigger, of course, and that's good. Listen, we didn't really talk about it last time, but I wanted to invite you to come along with me to the next appointment. I'd love the support. It's been really helpful for me to have you there for the last two visits, and it makes me feel like I'm not doing this whole thing alone. I'll admit, the closer I get to the due date, the more nervous I feel. I really appreciate your being there with me. It's a big help."

She hoped that the track she had taken in putting him in the position of a teammate and supportive partner would make him feel that his presence was as needed and wanted as it really was. She hadn't been lying about the support being needed or herself being more nervous as the big day approached.

There was a red circle around the due date on her wall calendar in the kitchen, and at the end of her seventh month she had been looking at it with anticipation and gratitude for her time nearing its close, but as the days faded away and the big red circle grew ever nearer, she had begun to feel a little more panic than gratitude knowing that she was going to be facing it all on her own.

It was an intimidating inevitability, and she had felt more at ease with Matthew around, as if she wasn't entirely on her own, and that he had taken some of the burden off of her. It had made her feel more at ease, and when she realized that, she'd decided to try to use that to compel him to keep coming to the appointments. He had to own up to his responsibilities, and she really wanted the support.

He hesitated a long moment before he answered her. "I wanted to apologize for last time. I know it was a little awkward there at the end... I didn't mean to withdraw so much, but it was a lot to try to take in, and I wasn't really expecting it. I... I don't know what to say other than I'm sorry. I feel like I left you kind of... deserted, and I didn't mean to do that. I apologize for leaving so abruptly like I did."

She heard him sigh heavily, and she felt sympathy warm her heart as she answered him. She knew he meant his apology genuinely, and she was ready and willing to accept it and move forward. "Thank you, Matthew, I really appreciate that.

I know it's hard for you right now, and I know you have a lot going on, both in your head and in your life, and this whole thing can't be easy to deal with. I'm just glad that you were there with me, and I'm glad you're giving me the wonderful support that you have. It's making such a big difference for me, and in turn, it's also making a difference for Charlie."

"Do you really think so?" he asked in a lighter voice, and she could have sworn that he sounded as if he was smiling.

"Yeah, I do. So, what do you say, do you think you could make it to this week's appointment?" she asked with a lilt of hope in her voice.

He answered her right away. "Yes, I'm sure of it. I can come. I'll admit, I kind of like being there. It's not like anything I've ever experienced before, and it's pretty surreal. I hadn't ever given it much thought before... everything that the mother goes through in carrying a child and giving birth to it, and going to the appointments with you has given me a perspective of it that I never could have imagined. It's really profound, actually, and I'm glad that I've been going." He laughed at himself then.

"All that just to say that, yes, I do want to go with you, and I'll be there to take you like we have been, if you want me to. It makes me feel better to drive you anyway," he admitted with a quiet chuckle.

She thanked him and gave him the information about the time of the next appointment. They talked a few minutes longer and then she said goodbye to him and they ended their phone call. Setting the cell phone down on the table, she wrapped both of her hands around her massive belly, rubbing it gently.

"Well, little one, your dad is coming to the next appointment. I have to tell you. I feel like we almost have this one in the bag. We're going to get him, Charlotte. We're going to get him for you soon." She smiled, knowing that it would happen, because she wasn't going to give up until it did, and Charlotte had a home to go to; her own home.

Her real home. That was going to happen, come hell or high water.

Two days later, Matthew showed up on her doorstep, just as he promised her that he would, and when she opened the door to him, she was delighted to see that he had brought a bouquet of flowers for her, and a card.

"What a sweet and thoughtful gesture!" she said, grinning as she buried her nose in the colorful bouquet. She set the vase on a table near the front door in the living room as he watched her and spoke to her.

"Well, it was the least I could do after deserting you last week. I just wanted to let you know how truly sorry I am that I left you like that. You don't deserve it. I'm going to make it up to you today, though!" he teased her with a wink and a smile.

She looked at him coyly then, out of response and with no thought to her manner. "You are? What else have you got up your sleeve?" she wondered curiously.

He shook his head just a little. "Don't you worry about it. As long as you don't already have plans for today, you'll be all set. Do you… already have plans for today?" There was a hint of panic and worry in his voice and she laughed at him for thinking of a plan, whatever it was that he was planning, without having checked with her first to know if she was free. She reasoned that it made sense that she would be free, but it didn't make it any less funny that he was so worried about respecting her time almost too late.

"I'm free," she answered back with a giggle. "I don't get to know what's going on?"

"Not right away," he answered, looking at her with a sidelong grin as he drove them to the doctor's office. She noticed as they were sitting together in the waiting room, that he was much more comfortable than he had been at the obstetrician's before, and she wondered if he was just getting used to it, or if she made him feel at ease. She hoped that it was both, but more so that he was at ease around her, just as she was around him. It felt friendlier between them, and as strange as it was to her to feel that change, she liked it.

River Lea was surprised when, during the course of the exam, Matthew looked at her with some shyness as he gave her a slight smile. The baby was moving around on the monitor beside them, and he was watching everything that it did with fascination.

"Would it be all right if I felt the baby moving?" he asked hesitantly.

She nodded and grinned back at him, so glad to hear him ask for that connection of his own accord. "Yes, Matthew, I think that would be nice." She reached for his hand and took it in hers, placing it palm down on the bare skin of her stomach.

Charlie responded right away, moving and pushing against her father's touch, and River Lea couldn't help but be delighted to see Matthew's giddy reaction to it. The moment that they shared between them felt warm and special, and she found herself cherishing it.

The doctor told them that the baby was doing very well, but that they still had some time before River Lea was going to be ready to give birth to Charlie. He was pleased to see the baby's growth and development, and he told them about the changes that were taking place with her, and what would be coming in the days ahead of them leading up to the birth.

Matthew paid close attention to it, asking questions and listening to everything that was said, and River Lea found herself hoping that it was because he was leaning more toward taking an interest in being the father he needed to be.

The pleasantness between them continued as they left the doctor's appointment, and Matthew helped her into the car. When he was sitting in it beside her, she looked over at him and raised one brow.

"So, what is it that we're going to be doing now? What was the secret that you were keeping before when you picked me up?" She hadn't said a word about it, but her patience had worn out.

He chuckled a little and nodded his head. "Okay, okay. I can tell you now." He paused a moment for effect and then glanced over at her and smiled. "I'm taking you to a day spa to get a full-body massage. I thought it might be nice for you to be pampered… considering how uncomfortable you must be feeling. I mean… you look great, but you look like you might just be a little uncomfortable, and that's to be expected."

She stared at him, and her lips parted slightly, though no sound came from her right away. "You're kidding… you're… you're taking me to a spa? I get to have a massage?" A smile spread over her face and she giggled a little and clapped her hands. "Really? I can't believe it! No one has ever done anything like that for me before! Thank you!"

He smiled and nodded again, giving his shoulders a shrug. "It's the least I can do. I mean…" he looked over at her swollen body again and a quiet sigh escaped him, "I just want you to be comfortable."

Knowing that he must be feeling some semblance of guilt, she decided not to take that part of the conversation any further, but instead to just enjoy the excitement of being spoiled while she had the chance.

River Lea had never seen anything like the spa that he took her into. It was the most luxurious place she had ever been. Right away she was impressed not only with how it all looked, but also with the friendly and attentive staff; it felt to her like every one of them wanted nothing more than to please her and make her feel like a queen.

Matthew told her that he would wait for her, and he made himself comfortable in a well-appointed lounge. The staff took her to a special scented steam bath, and then wrapped her in a thick terry cloth robe and escorted her to the room where she would be massaged. It was designed with a Japanese theme, and all of it was centered around relaxation.

Light flute music played softly in the background, a rock waterfall stood in one corner and the gentle flow of a moderate stream of water poured subtly down the stones. There were bamboo plants, a Japanese changing screen, and dim lights that gave the room a peaceful ambiance. She loved the look and feel of it, but she loved the massage she received more than anything else. It was two hours long, and done by a woman who took her time moving healing and strong hands over River Lea's body.

By the time it was over, River Lea was sure that she had never felt so relaxed in her entire life, and more than that, she knew she had never been so spoiled. She was blissful when she finally made her way into the lounge where Matthew was waiting for her.

He had been given snacks and tea, and was sitting in a large massage chair, working on his tablet. He looked up when she came in, and he gave her a big smile. "How was it? Are you feeling all right?"

She gave her head a slow shake of disbelief. "I have never felt so good in my life. I feel like I'm not even walking… like I'm floating along on a cloud and my feet aren't even touching the ground. I loved it so much. I don't know how I could ever thank you for that." She sighed happily as he stood up and walked with her out of the spa.

He laughed a little. "They are very nice. I'm so glad that you enjoyed it, and just knowing it did you so much good is thanks enough." He was thoughtful a moment and then looked over at her as they walked to the car. "I'll tell you what; I'll call them and set up a weekly massage for you for the next two months. You know, just to help you get your body back to where it was before. I'm sure it will help you."

She blinked at him in surprise. "You don't have to do that! I will be just fine."

He shrugged. "Really, it's no big deal. I'll be glad to do it, and I want to do it. So… I guess, just enjoy it as much as you did today, and that will be thanks enough." He smiled again and she decided to let it go and just be grateful for it, because she wasn't about to say no to getting another massage like she'd gotten. She thanked him once more and he nodded in acquiescence, but that was the end of it.

As she looked out of the window of the car, taking in all of the scenery around them as they drove back to her house, she realized that they were becoming friends, and she also realized that she liked it that way. He was a good man, even if he was uncertain about what he wanted to do with the situation regarding his fatherhood.

Turning her gaze back over to him, she felt a boldness rise up in her and she decided to go with it. "Matthew, I'd like to cook dinner for you tomorrow night at my place, to thank you for everything. What do you think? Are you able to come over tomorrow night?"

He looked surprised and when he replied, it was with a humble and soft manner. "I… yes, I would like that. Thank you," he answered, giving her another smile, and she knew that he was feeling the friendship growing between them as well.

Chapter Four

Gibby and River Lea walked through the small neighborhood marketplace together, laughing and talking about his latest dating stories with his friend Brad. She listened to him and looked over the stands of produce, picking up pieces of fruit and vegetables here and there as they went, filling the small basket hanging on her arm.

He grinned and sighed happily as he told her all about the fun times that Brad and he had been sharing, and as she watched him, seeing the changes that were coming over him, she realized something that took her a little by surprise, and warmed her heart enormously.

"You're falling for him! Look at you!" she said in a soft voice, her eyes steady on him. "You're falling in love!"

Gibby laughed and turned his head away from her, giving a slight shrug. "Maybe. I keep trying not to; I keep telling myself that he's just fun, and that we get along really well and that all the butterflies are just the newness of it, but I think you might be right. I think maybe I might be falling for him."

She gave her head a shake. "So… wouldn't that be a good thing if you two fell for each other? Wouldn't that make you happy? It seems like something you would really try to reach for. I would want you to be happy. I want the best for you; you know, someone to make you this blissful all the time, or at least most of the time. If you found someone who makes you feel like this whenever you talk about them or think about them, and they genuinely like you back as much as you like them, wouldn't you want to fall for them?"

He shrugged his shoulders and lifted his head to look at her directly. "Well… yes and no. I wasn't looking for a relationship; this just kind of fell in my lap. I think it's wise to take my time with it and make sure that it's right. There's no rush. I'm just enjoying it as it comes."

River Lea eyed him carefully and considered what he was saying. "You're pretty smart to look at it that way… you know, to be careful about it and take your time with it. Rushing in never really did anything good for anyone." She walked over to him and slipped her free hand through his arm.

"I just want you to be happy. You're my best friend and I love you. I love that you're doing fine on your own, but I think this guy makes you even happier." She gave him a wink and he grinned back at her.

"Well, we'll see how it goes." He looked around then and seemed to notice for the first time just what she was filling her basket with. Frowning he tipped his head and reached his hand over to the basket, pulling it to him slightly and peering into it.

"What's all this for? You don't usually buy this much food. Is that baby starving you to death?" He looked at her with some mild concern.

She laughed at him and shook her head. "No, the baby isn't starving me." She didn't know why she suddenly felt a little self-conscious answering his question, but her nerves tingled a little at the ends as she spoke it aloud.

"Matthew is coming over for dinner tonight," she said quietly and simply, turning her attention to a stack of avocados near them.

Gibby blinked at her. "Matthew….? As in the baby's father Matthew?" he looked at her in astonishment. He was quiet for a moment as he considered what she said and he continued in a curious voice. "Why is he coming over for dinner? Is this part of your ploy to help him become more attached to his daughter?"

Looking up at him, River Lea gave him a nod and a smile. "Yeah, that's most of it. There is a little more. He's a really nice guy and he's been really sweet to me this last week, and I wanted to do something nice in return for him, so I'm making dinner for him to thank him, and I'm hoping to get him more attached to this baby of his that I'm packing around. So, it's a twofold project, I guess."

He hummed quietly a moment as he regarded his friend, and for a brief minute she felt as if she was under some kind of surveillance, but then he nodded and looked away, and the nervousness in her evaporated.

"So what are you making for dinner?" he asked nonchalantly, shifting his eyes back to the basket on her arm.

She looked into the small basket herself and began to describe the meal that she was making. Gibby gave it some consideration and offered a few other thoughts on what she could make to pair with what she was already going to cook. River Lea liked his suggestions and the two of them went off in search of other pieces to add to the meal.

He didn't say anything else about her dinner guest, but she couldn't get the nagging feeling out of the back of her mind that made her wonder if she was looking forward to Matthew's company a little more than she ought to be. He was the father of the baby she was carrying, and a new friend, and that was all; and she told herself that she shouldn't feel any kind of nervousness or anticipation about his visit, but somewhere deep in her, it was there.

River Lea said goodbye to her best friend, who wished her luck and a good time with Matthew before he was on his way, and she went home to get dinner ready for the evening. She made the salad and put it in the refrigerator, and then set the meat into a dish in the oven to cook slowly.

That done, she thought she might change her clothes for the evening, and she went upstairs to her room to change into a pretty sundress that she felt like she looked good in. It was light and airy; all white cotton that clung to her curves, and the baby, and floated around the rest of her like a summer breeze. She fixed her makeup and dabbed on a little perfume, not wanting to smell like the meal she had just prepared for them.

Giving herself a final glance in the mirror, she smiled when she saw the reflection in the glass of her body and how pretty she was, especially with the baby belly rounded out in front of her. A nod of satisfaction, and she went downstairs to finish preparing the meal and the dining space on the table on the back porch for dinner.

It was a beautiful evening and she knew they would enjoy eating outside on the back deck, overlooking the ocean. She set a simple but lovely table for them with fresh flowers, pretty dishes, and lavender iced tea.

She was just going back in to check on dinner when she heard a knock at the front door. She felt her heart jump and beat a little faster as she walked over to it and pulled the door open with a smile. He was standing there with his own wide smile and a beautiful bouquet of flowers. He stepped in through the doorway and handed them to her, and she thanked him as she took them, pressing her nose into their soft petals to breathe them in and enjoy them for a moment.

"These are lovely! Thank you so much," she told him happily. "Come in. Dinner is just about finished." She turned and led the way into the bright kitchen overlooking the back deck and the ocean, and he followed her.

"This is a wonderful home. I like it. It's welcoming and warm." He paused a moment as he looked around the kitchen and then down at her. "Just like you... I guess. That makes sense. Of course it would reflect who you are."

She laughed and reached for a vase to put the flowers into, but she couldn't quite get to where it was on a high shelf. He saw that she was having trouble and went to her, standing just beside her, and reached up to grasp it easily. He lifted it from the shelf and set it carefully in her hand and she looked at up at him with a cute grin and took it from him.

"Thanks! I can't quite seem to get to that top shelf anymore. Maybe in another couple of months when I'm back to normal." She giggled a little bit and set the vase in the sink to run water into it. River Lea took a pair of kitchen shears and began to trim the bottoms of the flowers off to freshen them before setting them into the vase as it filled.

He watched her quietly as she worked and it felt comfortable between them; much the same to her as it felt when she was with Gibby, yet different somehow. There was something else that she felt between them that she couldn't quite identify. She hadn't ever felt it before. It was good, and she liked it, but it was strange to her.

She got the flowers arranged in the vase and carried the vase outside to the table, and then the two of them carried dinner out to the table and sat down to eat together.

He gazed around him at the picturesque view and drew in a deep breath, letting it out slowly. She could see his whole body relax and it pleased her. She hoped that it would help him become more receptive to her plan of talking to him about taking his daughter home with him, when she brought the subject up later in the evening.

"This is incredibly beautiful," he said to her as he took it all in. "What a wonderful place to live."

She nodded in agreement. "I love it. I was lucky to be able to get this place. My grandmother left me some money, and I used it to invest in this property so that I could live here and so that I could have some financial security in a home I own. Plus… I just love living here; it's perfect."

"That's good thinking." He looked at her with appraising eyes. "It's a smart move. I always say, anytime someone gets money, they should buy dirt. It's one of the best investments out there."

She laughed and looked out at the ocean. "I invested in dirt, but my love is the sea. That's my whole life right out there in front of us."

He laughed with her at the irony of it, but then a curious look overtook his face and he regarded her with interest.

"Is that your only love? The sea?" His voice grew quieter.

She blinked and tipped her head as she looked back at him. "What do you mean?"

Matthew drew in another big breath and let it out slowly. "Well… I just… I wondered if you happen to be in a relationship with anyone… significant. I mean… you're a beautiful woman. You're smart and capable. You're dedicated and strong. You're quite a lady, and you're young. This is typically an age for young women when they are more often in romantic relationships with men.

You're in a different kind of situation, though. You're pregnant... and I could see how that would deter a lot of men who might otherwise be interested in you. Are you already in a relationship with someone, or are you waiting until after the baby is born?" he asked, eyeing her carefully.

She hadn't been expecting the question and it caught her a little off guard. She reached for her lavender iced tea and took a long drink of it, setting the glass back on the table before she answered him.

"I'm not in a relationship. I actually haven't been in one for a long time. There was a guy I saw throughout high school, but when we graduated, we went separate ways. I have dated a little in college, but nothing serious. I have been really focused on my goals and what I want to do. I've been so busy with school that I haven't actually given it a lot of thought.

Then there was this circumstance with your daughter, and that became a priority for me, alongside my education." She shook her head thoughtfully and gave a shrug. "I guess you're right about it deterring men… I certainly don't get hit on like I used to by guys who were interested in me, but I wasn't taking them very seriously at all to begin with.

I've been concentrating on getting my degree and graduating, and then getting into my career. I guess romance took a back seat to all of that." She was surprised that he had even thought to ask her about her romantic situation; it was something that she didn't think about much on her own, or talk about with anyone else. She was focused on her education and her future career, and that was it.

He was quiet as he ate, looking as though he was considering all that she said. She hoped that he was thinking about taking his child with him when she was born, and giving River Lea her life back. She was anxious to get to it, and spend all of her time and energy on graduating and working in the field she loved so much.

The subject of conversation changed and took a lighter, easier turn, and they took their time eating and enjoying the sunset together. When twilight began to fall, they carried the dishes back into the kitchen and he helped her clean them up and load the dishwasher. Just as they finished up the dishes, she stopped and reached her hand to her stomach and he looked at her sharply.

"Are you okay? Is the baby all right?" he asked with a note of panic in his voice.

She laughed a little and nodded. "Yes, we're both fine. She's just moving around. It's her dinner time now." She looked up at him and found his brown eyes locked on hers worriedly. Without thinking about it, she reached for his hand and drew it to her belly, pressing his palm flat against the hard surface of it.

Charlie moved and turned beneath his touch, giving him well placed kicks. At the feel of her, all of the concern on his face melted away and it was replaced with a smile that spread wide. They stood close together feeling the baby move, both of them wrapped in a blissful silence as they looked at each other and shared a gaze that spoke of the natural magic they were both experiencing.

He shook his head slowly when Charlie calmed down and stopped moving so much, and he let his hand fall away from River Lea, but his eyes stayed on her. "That was amazing. Does she do that very often?" he asked, almost in a hush.

River Lea nodded. "Yes, she does that several times throughout the day. She's a spunky little thing. Very full of life and personality. She's a special little girl."

Matthew didn't say anything. He looked to River Lea as if he couldn't really say anything. She saw emotion churning in his eyes, and she knew that it was no time to speak. There was a tidal wave of change and understanding passing between them.

It looked for a moment like it might be too much for Matthew to take, and there was a moment when she thought she saw him surrender to it, and she knew that he needed some support.

She reached her arms up and took him into them, embracing him gently and holding him close. He did not hesitate to hug her in return, and they stood there together in each other's arms, in a profound silence that was full of so much more than nothing. She felt his warm cheek on hers, and his breath on her neck as he breathed her in deeply. She could feel his heartbeat pulsing rapidly, and in a moment of unexpected connection, she closed her eyes and let herself feel everything was happening on a deep and personal level; much deeper than she had let herself feel with any man for a long time.

He whispered softly into her ear. "Thank you so much. This is so… incredible." Slowly he moved his mouth from her ear to her cheek, and she felt his lips close gently on it, kissing her tenderly once, and then again a second time, and she could not stop the gasp of breath that she drew in as everything in her body tingled and felt as though it had just come alive.

Matthew held her a moment longer, and his breath on her cheek seemed shallow. She didn't open her eyes until he let her go, pulling his arms from her and taking a deep breath. She blinked and looked up at him, realizing that she needed her own big breath just then. They gazed at one another in the stillness around and between them, and then both of them smiled, slowly and sweetly.

"It is pretty incredible," she agreed with him. She began to turn slightly, feeling her heartbeat pick up a little as his eyes stayed on her, and she glanced back at him. "I'm going to go out and get the flowers. I'll be right back." He nodded once, and she turned and walked back out to the deck.

The cool air felt good on her and she laughed a little, thinking that it must have just been too long since any man but Gibby had hugged her. With a shake of her head, she picked up the flowers and brought them back into the kitchen.

Matthew looked as if he was himself again, and nothing felt awkward between them. He was leaning his back against the counter, and he pushed himself up off of it when she came back into the room. "This has been a really fun evening. I had a good time being here." He let a breath out and glanced around the room before looking back at her. "I should probably be going, though."

She smiled at him and walked with an unhurried pace out of the kitchen, through the living room, and toward the front door, and he followed her.

"It has been a lot of fun. I'm glad that you came here and we got to have this time together. Thank you!" She opened the door for him and turned to look up at him again, thinking to herself that it had been one of the best evenings she'd had in a long while.

He wrapped her in another hug, though the second one felt slightly less intimate than the hug that they had just shared in the kitchen, and he let her go, looking down at her with a smile. "So, let me know about the next appointment, all right? I would like to go with you, if that's all right."

She nodded. "Absolutely. I'll give you a call. I'd be so glad to have you there."

He thanked her once more and bid her goodnight, and River Lea watched Matthew as he walked out to his car, turned when he reached it and gave her another wave, and then climbed into it and drove away. She didn't close the door until he was gone out of sight, and then she turned and walked back into her house, feeling almost as if she was walking on a cloud.

There was a strange and unfamiliar sensation in her, and she wondered how in the world Matthew's wife could have left him and what it was that went wrong for them. She thought of how he had said that their marriage had been cold for so long, and she found herself amazed by it. She couldn't begin to imagine anything being cold with him.

She slept deeply that night, and when she woke in the morning, she opened her eyes feeling as if she was filled with happiness. There was a smile on her face as she readied for the day, and after she ate breakfast, she picked up her cell phone to call Gibby. She had promised him that she would give him a full report from the night before and her dinner with Matthew.

He was happy to hear from her, and was anxious to know how it had all gone.

"Well?" he asked with little patience, "How was it?"

She chuckled, knowing just the expression he had on his face. "It was fun! We had a nice time. I made the dinner and it came out really well. He showed up and brought me a beautiful bouquet of flowers, and we talked a lot. We ate out on the deck and watched the sunset, and then he helped me with the dinner dishes."

She heard Gibby breathe a sigh of relief. "Well, thank heaven. Here I've been wondering all night, and it was the first thing I thought of this morning. I was about to call you myself to see how it was, but I know that you need your rest. So, what else? Did you talk to him about taking the baby home?"

Pressing her lips together for a moment, she rolled her eyes a little and shook her head. "No, I guess I didn't. There was one thing, though. After the dishes, he was standing beside me in the kitchen and Charlie started moving. I put his hand on my belly and he got to feel her, and I think it really affected him. I am so sure that our plan is working and that he's getting so much closer to changing his mind." She thought back over the moment they had shared the night before, and happiness, like warmth, spread through her.

"If you could have seen him—how he reacted and what it was like for him to feel her moving again, and how it felt to us both… you'd have been so surprised. He wasn't at all like he was the first night I talked to him at the restaurant. Not at all. I can see changes in him, and I'm telling you, I think he's going to want to take our little Charlotte home." She was smiling wide by the time she stopped speaking.

Gibby was quiet for a beat. "So… you were kind of feeling this special moment with him, too?" he asked with some hint of hesitation and no small amount of curiosity in his voice.

River Lea's mind and thoughts were on Matthew from the night before, and she didn't catch the subtle tone in his voice. "Yeah, I guess so. It was really wonderful. We just kind of… connected… in this amazing way. It was as if the three of us were all connected together, and he and I both loved it. I've never felt anything like that before."

She frowned then and rubbed her fingertip over her chin thoughtfully. "You know, I was thinking about it after he left, but it's so weird to me that his wife could have left him and that their marriage wasn't working. He's such a great guy! He's so thoughtful and sweet. He's generous and kind. He's just… wonderful… and let's be honest; the man is beautiful and wealthy. I mean… how could it not have worked for them? What in the world

121

did she ever let him go for? I'll tell you, if he was mine, I'd hold on pretty tight to him. She must be out of her mind."

There was silence for a moment on the other end of the phone line. "Uh huh," Gibby said slowly. "You wouldn't let him go."

River Lea shook her head. "No. I wouldn't. I can't figure out what her deal was, but she sure left him a mess with this baby and his hurt heart. I don't think he's too terribly torn up about it. He said it's been hard between them for a couple of years, and so I think this isn't a new heartache for him. I think it's been building for a while, and he's been trying to salvage it, but it was just too late.

Now she's gone and he is facing fatherhood alone. I think he was just scared to death about it, and a little lost, and I think now that he's starting to get used to the idea of Charlotte... you know, seeing her on the monitor at the appointments, and feeling her move, and I think he worries about her, well... I think our plan is working and it's going to wind up changing him enough that he will take her home."

"Hmm," Gibby hummed quietly. He was silent for a little longer before speaking again. "River…" he began and hesitated.

"Yeah?" she asked, still not quite hearing the suggestive tone of his voice.

"Are you… uh… are you developing some feelings for this guy? Like… more than friend feelings?" he asked, still trying to remain subtle with her while getting his point across.

Her eyes widened as she finally caught what it was that he was saying to her. "Oh! Oh my gosh! Gibby! No! No… there's nothing like that. How could you even think that? No! No…" she took a breath and shook her head. "I just… I just mean that things are… um… they're nice between us. That's all. They're… things are good between him and I and we are becoming friends. That's all. There's nothing else going on. We probably won't even talk after the baby is born and he takes her home. That will be that. He'll have her. I'll be paid. I'll get back to school. It'll all be over with. That's it."

"Uh huh," Gibby said, and she heard the disbelief in his voice loud and clear that time.

"Gibby, when I said I wouldn't let him go, I just meant that if I was her I would not have walked out on him and their marriage and their baby because he's a good guy. I didn't mean that I wanted to be in any part of that or that I want him." She wasn't sure why she suddenly felt so defensive, but she did.

"I can't even believe that you brought that up or suggested it! What are you thinking? He's not… and I'm certainly not… um… interested in anything together as a… not at all! I can't believe you even said that! That's not what I meant at all." Her tone grew slightly huffy.

He sighed with uncertainty. "Okay, whatever you say my dear. I'm just hearing a lot of…

connection… and I haven't heard you talk about any guy like that before, so I just wondered."

She frowned and furrowed her brows. "Well, it's not that kind of connection. I'm just trying to persuade him to take his baby girl when I give birth to her. This is business. That's all. You're probably just hearing pregnancy hormones and mistook it for something else entirely, which is isn't… um… anything else. It's just business. That's it. We're kind of friends now, but that is definitely all that there is."

"Okay. No need to get so fired up. I was just asking. Just… wondering. I haven't heard you like this before." His tone lightened, and she felt like he might have let it go. He changed the subject then, and she felt relief wash through her as he started talking about him and Brad, and after that, the possibility of the two of them going to the zoo together that day to enjoy the sunny warm weather.

She agreed to the zoo trip, and when she hung up, she felt a little sorry for having gotten so defensive with him about his questions and suppositions. She realized that the things she had said about Matthew and his marriage and how she felt about it all might be easily misconstrued, and she apologized to him later when they met up. He waved it off as if it was nothing, but she thought she could feel him watching her more closely throughout the day whenever the subject of Matthew came up.

River Lea called him a few days later, and told Matthew when the next appointment was. He promised to be there to pick her up and take her to it, and she found herself looking forward to seeing him and spending the time with him, though she told herself that she was only feeling so glad about it because she would have another chance to try to get him more interested in his daughter, and want to take the baby home with him.

In the two days that passed between her calling him to tell him about the baby appointment, and the moment that he was standing on her doorstep, she thought about him so many times that she couldn't have counted them. He was on her mind when she woke up, and several times throughout the day. He was on her mind every time the baby moved, and every time she heard something that reminded her of something he'd said. She thought of him as she shopped, as she cooked, and as she sat on her back deck. She found herself looking through her phone and reading the few texts that they had sent to one another, and then rereading them, smiling to herself as she did.

By the time he came to take her to the baby appointment, she was excited to see him, and she hugged him tightly for a moment before letting him go. He held her back, just as tightly, and let her go with a grin before walking her to his car.

He asked her how she was feeling and how little Charlie was doing, and she told him about the previous few days and how they had passed. She explained how she was feeling alright, but how it seemed that Charlie was sitting lower in her body than she had been, and how the baby wasn't moving around quite as much as she had been before.

She told Matthew that she thought that the pregnancy was coming close to being over, and a mixture of panic, anticipation, excitement, and fear played out on his face, though he didn't say anything. He did look over at her several more times before they reached the doctor's office.

The appointment seemed to go as the others had; they watched the baby, they checked her heartbeat and all of the numbers, and the doctor said that the baby was closer, but that they still had some more time, and Matthew looked more than a little relieved to get the news update.

When they left the appointment, she noticed that he was as close to her as he had been the last time they had seen each other, but that he was much more quiet and pensive, and she wondered what was going on his mind, though she wasn't sure if she should ask. She didn't have long to wait before she found out.

He was driving away from the doctor's office when he looked over at her with a lowered brow and a serious expression. "Would it be all right if we went to get some coffee and visited?" he asked hopefully.

She felt her heartbeat pick up its pace some, and her nerves began to tingle a little. "Yes, of course. That would be nice," she answered him, still wondering, but willing to wait to let him speak in his own time.

He took them to a nearby coffee shop and they sat together in a private booth. She sipped the hot tea she'd chosen and he wrapped his hands around the coffee mug in front of him, and looked at her intently.

"I've been giving a lot of thought to this whole situation, and having spent so much time with you and Charlotte has really given me a different kind of perspective. I've been feeling very… close to her. I feel like I have a duty to her and an obligation.

Well…" he sighed, "I feel like it's much more than that. Just… seeing her and feeling her… she's so much more real to me than she was before. I mean, of course I knew she was real, and I wanted her when Amil and I first made the decision to have her, but I just wasn't around at all during the pregnancy, and I think I felt unattached to her."

He shook his head. "Now that I've spent all of this time with her and..." he hesitated a moment, "...and with you, it's so much more real. There's been a big impact on me, and I understand what you were saying before on the beach about how she could really heal me and make me happy, and how I owe it to her to be there for her as her father."

A smile curved over his mouth. "Actually, she is already making me happy, and I didn't know what I was missing out on before... before I spent time seeing her and.... I guess connecting with her. She's in there, and I know what she looks like, and I know what her heartbeat sounds like, and I have felt her move against my hand and kick me, and... well... that's my little girl in there." He leaned back against the seat and looked at River Lea with genuine excitement and happiness.

"I feel like it would be best if I took her home to live with me. She's my daughter and she needs me, and I need her just as much. You were right about it." He shook his head and let out a long slow sigh. "I should have listened to you right from the start. Thank goodness you didn't give up on her or me, and you didn't take the original offer that I made to you that night in the restaurant, when I was so ready to give up my own child.

I feel awful that it ever crossed my mind; like I was letting her down, and letting myself down, and even letting you down. I'm just really lucky that you were smart enough and strong enough to help me see just what it was that I was about to lose and give up before it was too late." He blinked back a tear and smiled warmly at her River Lea, and she grinned back at him as her heart raced in her chest, and she suddenly felt as if she had just won the biggest race of her life.

"She will be the best thing that ever happened to you, and you are giving yourself that gift. You're giving both you and her a chance at real love and happiness that will last all of your life. There's no gift more precious." She reached her hand across the table to take his and hold it, and they curled their fingers together as they held hands.

"I have you to thank for that," he said with a genuine smile. "I don't know that I can ever really thank you enough or repay you for what you've taken the time to show me… stopping me from making the biggest mistake of my life in letting her go."

River Lea just shrugged and gave him a nod.

He looked away from her then for a moment, and when his eyes met hers again, he leaned in closer to her and lowered his voice a little. "There is something else, though," he said with a humbled expression.

She grew curious and leaned in toward him, meeting him partway. "What is it?" she asked in a soft voice.

He drew a deep breath and sighed, furrowing his brow slightly. "Well, I'm not ready to take her home at all. I mean… emotionally I'm ready to, but that's it. There's nothing for her at my home. Nothing at all. My ex was going to set up the nursery, but she never got started on it, and then she left, and I thought I wouldn't keep the baby, so I never started it, and now there's nothing there.

We're down to the wire on this, and I have almost no time to prepare for her, and no one to help me get ready, and I know nothing about what I will need, or what she will need, or what to buy, or even where to go to buy it! I'm totally lost on this, and I have no clue where to start with any of it." He pressed his lips together in a solid line and then relaxed them and breathed out a shallow breath.

"I was wondering… I was hoping… that, if you aren't opposed to it…. I thought maybe you could help me with some of it. Maybe you could show me what I need to do to get ready for her to come home with me. What do you think?" He looked as if he had just asked her the biggest favor he had ever asked anyone, and she suppressed a laugh to think that he had not looked as nervous about asking her to carry the baby the first time they'd met, as he did sitting there asking her to help him prepare for the little girl to be taken to his home.

The look of lost apprehension on his face melted her heart. There was no way that she could turn him down and know that he was going to try to take Charlotte home and wouldn't be prepared for the baby's needs right away.

She nodded and smiled at him. "Of course I'll be glad to help you! When were you thinking of getting things ready?"

He laughed a little. "Today… if you can. We don't have very much time."

River Lea laughed in return. "Yeah, I can help you today. Actually, I don't have anything going on between now and whenever she's born, so I will be able to help you as much as you need. I would want her to have all that she needs as well. We'll get a nursery set up and make sure it's all ready for her when she goes home."

She paused and gave him a genuine smile. "Matthew, I want to tell you how glad I am to hear you say that you're going to take her home with you. It really is the very best thing that you can you for yourself and for her. She's your daughter, and the bond that the two of you will share will be amazing, and it will last all of your life. Are you planning on hiring a nanny to help you?"

He sighed and raked his hand through the brown waves of his hair. "I think I'm going to, but I don't know how or where to find a nanny; I'd want the best, of course, but I wasn't quite sure how to get that figured out as well." He shrugged and she realized that he didn't have anything lined up for the baby that was moving around inside of her just then. She knew that he was going to need all of the help that she could give him, and something in her just couldn't let him fail; not with the baby girl she was carrying.

She gave him a sympathetic smile and reached across the table to take his hand in hers. "I'll help you with everything. Don't worry about it. We'll get the nursery set up together, and it'll be ready for her."

His face flushed with relief and he sighed as he smiled and leaned back against his seat. "I'm really grateful for that, River Lea. So grateful. I can't tell you how much it means to me to have any kind of help at all, and especially help from you. I mean, you're doing so much of this anyway; or all of it, really.

You're carrying her and bringing her into the world, and I feel like there's nothing I can ever do or give you that would repay you for that. Then you go above and beyond the call and help me through the last month, trying to get me back on track being a father to the daughter you're giving me, and then offering to help me with her nursery and getting ready for her.

I just...." He shook his head and pressed his lips together in a smile. "I'm immeasurably grateful. I have so much to thank you for."

He looked deeply into her eyes and the gratitude that he felt was conveyed to her. She felt as if she was glowing with happiness from the inside, and she was so immersed in it, that it seemed as if it was overflowing all through her.

They left the coffee shop and he took her from there directly to a series of stores where they proceeded to buy baby furniture, paint, nursery décor, stuffed animals, books, toys, and everything from blankets and bottles to clothes and bath items.

Matthew was overwhelmed at all of the things that she showed him that babies needed or were useful and helpful with any infant. At first he worried that they were getting too many things, and then he worried that they weren't getting enough, and she remained patient with him, helping him through all of it as best she could.

Hours of shopping later, and after a stop to share an early dinner at a restaurant, he drove her to his home. She expected it to be in Silicon Valley, but he told her that was where he worked. His home was on the coast, thirty minutes north of hers. She was surprised about that, but delighted when she found out, and incredulous when she saw the home itself.

It was a multi-level home built into a hillside directly over the ocean. There was a pathway to a private beach behind the house, and a long private driveway that led to the main road. The home itself was enormous, and though large, it was also welcoming and open. There was a four-car garage and large arches over an outdoor foyer. The front door was a doublewide oak entrance that led into an interior foyer, as big as the one outside.

There were archways in the foyer that led off to different rooms; a spacious living room, a library, a dining room, and a wide staircase that led up to other levels of the house. It looked as though it had been professionally designed by a top notch interior decorator. He walked her around some of the house before he took her upstairs to show her where the nursery would be.

They walked down the hallway of the second story and he explained that his room, which was the biggest, connected to a smaller room where he wanted the nursery to be. The smaller room was empty and seemed to her like a shell, waiting for life to be brought into it.

The nursery had big windows which let in lots of bright sunshine, as well as a walk-in closet and its own small bathroom. The windows overlooked the hill beside the house, and the sea beyond that. She smiled wide as she stood in the room and looked around. She was elated that the little child in her was going to be living in a place as beautiful as the one she was standing in. It made her absolutely positive that she had done just the right thing in pushing Matthew to take his daughter home with him.

He walked up behind her and stood near her, looking at her as she gazed out of the window. He spoke and his voice was soft. "What do you think of it? Do you think this will work? Do you think this will make a good nursery for her?"

She could hear the uncertainty in his voice, but more than that, she heard hope and it made her smile to know that he was committing himself to his child the way that he was. She turned her head and looked up at him.

"Yes, I think this is going to be perfect. I think she's going to be a lucky little girl, and you are going to be very lucky to have her here, too. This is a dream nursery, and I'm sure she'll love it." She turned and faced him fully then. "We just have to get it ready for her!" She gave him a nod and he raised his eyebrows and let out a slow breath.

"Well, I feel like we bought everything she could ever need for her first year. Shall we start getting it ready?" He looked at her expectantly, and she grinned at him.

"Yes. Let's do this!" she agreed as she followed him back down to the car to help him bring in as much as she could.

Minutes became hours, and the hours found them working together to build the crib and wash sheets and bottles, set up a toy box and a book case, secure shelving to walls and piece together a mobile, wash and fold all of the baby clothes and blankets, set up a rocking chair, a bassinet, a diaper changing station, and décor in the room.

They got much of it finished, laughing and struggling through it together, helping each other with the tricky parts, and making it all come together as much as they could with as little time as they had. She yawned late into the evening and he saw her do it.

Worry shaded his brown eyes and he walked over to her and set a hand on her arm. "Are you tired? Should I take you home?" he asked in concern.

She sighed and her eyes moved over the room, taking in all that they had done, but seeing that they still had quite a bit to do. She tipped her head thoughtfully and then looked up at him questioningly with her sea blue eyes.

"I am tired, but we do have so much to work on here. Would it be all right if I laid down for a nap for a little while? When I wake up I can come back in here and help you with this some more," she offered pleasantly.

He looked doubtful for a moment. "I could take you home, and we could do this tomorrow or another day." He hesitated. "You're welcome to stay here, of course, but I don't want you to do too much."

She raised her eyebrows seriously and rubbed her hands over the massive mound of baby in her belly, which had sunk quite low. "I don't think we have time to put anything off. I want you to be able to have everything ready for Charlie when she comes home here, so I think it would be best if I just rest here for a little while and then we can pick this back up together in a bit. Would that be all right?"

Matthew cracked a little smile and nodded his head. "Yes, that would probably be best. You're right about her coming soon. We should have everything ready for her."

He walked toward the door that led to his bedroom then, and turned to look at her. "You could rest there in my room, and I'll just stay in here and work while you sleep, if that's okay."

She gave him a nod and he walked in with her to help her into his bed. It was made of mahogany wood; a huge, canopied, king-size bed that was laden with pillows and a thick comforter. She looked at it as if it was heaven just waiting for her to come lay down and rest.

River Lea climbed into it and moved around a bit until she was comfortable, and Matthew sat on the bed beside her. "Will this work? Is it comfortable?" he asked, looking over her as if he might be able to see anything that he could make better for her.

She nodded and smiled at him. "Charlie's moving… do you want to feel her?" she asked lightly.

He grinned and she took his hand and placed it on top of her stomach. The baby kicked and prodded and he chuckled, shaking his head. He looked up at River Lea in wonder and spoke softly. "It's so incredible... she's a little miracle, right in there. How in the world is that even possible? Isn't it amazing?"

A quiet laugh bubbled up from River Lea. "That's about the most true thing I've ever heard about pregnancy. They are little miracles, aren't they? It's incredible that they are even possible."

He lowered his eyes to her belly and gave it a gentle rub. "Charlie is going to be the best miracle of my life." His voice was soft and he smiled to himself before lifting his eyes to meet River Lea's. She was staring at him.

"You're calling her Charlie now... are you going to keep calling her that? You don't have to. I named her that after my grandmother. It's just what I've been calling her, but it's a little strange to hear you call her that. I do like it... but... you don't have to keep calling her that. You could name her anything," she said quietly as a little pinch of sadness tugged at her heart. She realized that she wasn't going to have a Charlie any longer, and the comprehension of it made her feel some sense of loss.

A smile slowly spread over his face and he reached his hand from River Lea's belly to her cheek. "You are the closest thing this baby has to a mother, and you've taken such good care of her this whole time, and you've looked out for her and me, making sure that she has this home to come to and that I will look after her as I should be.

You've done more than I ever expected you to do. You've been amazing, and I am humbled by your friendship and your dedication to this baby girl. I have given it some thought and if it's all right with you, I do want to call her Charlotte, or Charlie, just as you have been. That's... that's who she is to me now. I don't think I could call her anything else."

River Lea felt her heart swell with emotion, and her eyes grew wet with tears of happiness. She reached her hand up to cover Matthew's hand as it rested on her cheek, and she gave him a soft smile.

"Thank you. That means so much to me. I'm always going to love that," she almost-whispered.

His gaze connected with hers seemed to feel like a magnet, drawing them together, and he leaned toward her without pause or hesitation, and with the gentlest of touches, he pressed his lips to hers for a moment. It was a soft kiss, tender and sweet, and as he came to her, she didn't think she could breathe, but the moment she felt his lips warm against hers, she could not help but draw in a deep breath, just to try to steady herself.

Matthew opened his eyes briefly, staring down at her, and then lowered his mouth to hers again, 'kissing her more intently, once more, carefully, and then again with more depth. She kissed him in return, matching his movements, and when he parted her lips with his, tentatively touching his tongue to hers, she tasted him back as their kiss grew more fervent, until he moaned softly.

The sound of it seemed to break the spell of pleasure between them, and he broke the kiss abruptly, and leaned back up away from her. His eyes were wide and his mouth was still parted, open with breathlessness.

She stared at him and he gasped and looked away from her for a moment before returning his gaze to her. "I'm so sorry… I'm… God, I don't know what I was thinking. I didn't mean to… I'm so sorry," he said quietly, as his brow furrowed and a troubled expression overtook his face.

River Lea wasn't quite sure what to think. One minute they were talking and sharing a tender moment, and the next he was kissing her, and everything in her responded to it at the very first touch of his lips to hers. She had closed her eyes and felt warmth rush through her like a river freed from a dam. Her heart had begun to race in her, and as they tasted one another, all she could feel was a desire to taste more of him, and for him to be closer to her.

She hadn't been able to think at all as they had kissed, and the feel of all of it had been like a sweet dream to her, until the kiss had been broken. Her senses came to her, and she realized that it was not at all what was best for either of them, or for the baby.

"I'm sorry too," she told him, feeling a little guilty for enjoying it so much. "I didn't mean to... I don't know what came over me. Maybe... hormones?" She gave a weak laugh and he nodded and shrugged.

"I guess we just... let that go," he said humbly, and she agreed with a nod. He drew in a deep breath and let out a long sigh as he stood up and moved away from the bed, walking to the doorway. His hand rested on the door handle, and he looked back over his shoulder at her.

"Get some good rest," he told her in a tender voice, and then he walked out and closed the door behind him.

The room went dark and she closed her eyes after a minute, trying to convince herself to go to sleep; knowing how tired she was. As she laid there, her mind remained steady on the kiss that they had just shared, on every part of it, from the first touch to the last, and on everything she felt as it had happened.

She couldn't get it from her mind, and she realized that she didn't want to. As she drifted off to sleep, the only thing she was thinking about was the feel of his lips on hers, and how much she loved how it felt, and how she wished it could have continued.

When she woke hours later, she opened her eyes to see daylight shining throughout the room, and she drew in a sharp and panicked breath, pushing herself up in the bed, disoriented for a minute before she remembered where she was.

Smiling subtly, she remember the last thing that happened before she fell asleep and she raised her fingers to her lips and touched them where he had kissed her. Her smile widened and she felt her cheeks warm. It had been longer than she cared to remember since she had kissed anyone, and she was glad that it had happened, even if it shouldn't have.

River Lea climbed carefully out of the bed and after stopping in the bathroom to refresh herself and straighten the curls around her head, she walked into the nursery and stopped short not more than two steps into the doorway.

It was done. All of it. There was nothing else that needed to be taken care of. She looked around and thought to herself that she could just as easily have been looking at a model room for a magazine shoot.

She smiled as she looked in the corner for there in the rocking chair, fast asleep, was Matthew. She watched him a moment, smiling to herself at what a good man he was, and what a good father she knew that he would be, and then she walked over to him and woke him gently.

He opened his eyes in surprise and looked around, just as disoriented as she had been when she'd woken in his bed a short while before. He drew in a breath and stretched, arching his back and raising his hands over his head. It made the muscles in his chest swell for a moment and she found herself staring at them before she realized what she was doing and looked away. He was a well-built man, and sometimes when she looked at him, it was impossible not to notice.

Matthew stood up and looked around the room before his eyes found hers. "Well? How does it look? Do you think this will work? Is there anything missing that she needs?"

River Lea turned herself in a circle on the spot and looked at all of it as she shook her head. "No. I think it's perfect. This is absolutely perfect." She turned and looked back up at him. "You're ready!" she told him, and she could have sworn that she saw his face go pale for a minute.

Laughing, she reached a hand out to comfort him, laying it on his arm. "You're going to be fine. I promise. It's all going to work out just fine."

"I hope you're right." He gave his head a shake as he looked down at the floor and then back up at her. "In the meantime, I should probably get you home. You need some proper rest, and I have to get some things taken care of on my end."

He drove her back to her house and walked her to her doorway, hugging her tenderly for a long minute before he let her go. "Thank you so much for everything," he said with a smile. "You're amazing."

She laughed a little. "You're welcome. Thank you, too. You're pretty amazing yourself."

Then she turned and went inside, and he left, and she watched him drive up the road, telling herself that she had to stop thinking about his kiss, and how much she liked it when he took her in his arms and held her in his embrace.

He texted her intermittently throughout the next few days, checking on her to see if she needed anything, and sending her photos of things he'd bought for the nursery or the house or the car for the baby. She laughed to see how much he was getting into the idea of being a new dad, and how exciting it had become for him.

When she talked with Gibby, she didn't tell him about the kisses that she and Matthew had shared. She only told him about the two of them getting the nursery ready, and how he had turned himself around and was looking forward to bringing his daughter home. Gibby listened to her and watched her, saying aloud how good it was that things had gone the way they had hoped they would, but saying with his eyes that he was fairly certain that there was more going on than had originally been planned.

Chapter Five

A few more days passed, and she'd spent many hours of those days telling herself to stop thinking about him the way that she was. He crossed her mind so often that he was nearly always on it, and when it wasn't him on her mind, it was the little girl inside of her who was on her mind.

She was tremendously relieved to know that the girl she was carrying was going to go to such a good home, and that she would be loved and given the very best care. She talked to Charlie about it, telling her about the room that Matthew and she had readied for her, and the life that she was going to have with her dad. She told her how happy she would be, and how much she would love growing up in her home with Matthew.

River Lea fell asleep and dreamed of Charlie and Matthew one night, thinking of them as the night overtook her, and they stayed with her in her dreams all through the night. When she opened her eyes in the morning, she was smiling, and she felt as if every part of her had been immersed in happiness. Until she shifted her legs in the bed she was lying in, and a big gush of warm water flowed from her.

Panic nearly stopped her heart in her chest and her eyes flew open wide. She gasped and sat up as fast as she could in the bed. Throwing back the covers, she stared down at the sheets and her nightgown, and realized in a moment what it was that had happened. Her water had broken, and she knew that meant it was time for Charlie to come into the world.

With her heart racing, she reached over to the nightstand beside her and grabbed her cell phone. The first call she made was to Matthew. He answered after a couple of rings, and sounded as if he had been sleeping.

"Hello? River Lea? Are you all right?" he asked, his voice a little groggy.

She thought her heart might pound right out of her chest. She tried to catch her breath to speak. "I think I'm in labor. I think my water just broke." She said the words, even though hearing them still didn't make them feel real to her.

There was the briefest moment of silence at the other end of the line, and then she heard his voice and tone change completely. It was as if he was suddenly wide awake at his end. "I'll be right over!" he answered swiftly, and then there was silence. She frowned and looked at the phone in her hand. The call had ended.

She called Gibby and he answered with a questioning tone to his voice. "This is an early call for you... are you okay? Are you in labor?"

"I'm in labor," she replied. "I think I'm okay. I'm not sure how this is supposed to go... but I think my water just broke all over my bed."

"Okay, well, take it easy, just relax and breathe deep and I'll come right over. Don't panic, and don't try to get up and do anything. Just stay put, and I'll be right there," he told her seriously.

"Okay. Thanks, Gibby." She spoke in a hushed voice. They ended their call and she set the phone back on the bedside table and leaned back against her pillows, closing her eyes and breathing deep as she tried to relax herself. She reached her hands to her belly and rubbed it gently, talking to Charlie as she did so.

"It's going to be okay, kiddo. It's all going to be okay. This is your big day! You're going to come out in just a little while and meet us, and we are all so looking forward to meeting you!" She tried to smile and use an encouraging voice as she talked to the little one. Just then, a sharp pain began to pierce her lower back, and it stayed steady and strong for a long while. She tried to breathe through it, focusing and concentrating on her breathing until the pain subsided, and when it was gone, she opened her eyes and tried to talk herself through it.

"That wasn't so bad. That was all right. If that's as bad as it gets, we're going to be just fine," she promised herself, not entirely sure that that was as bad as it would get, but hoping for both hers and Charlie's sake that it was.

She laid in the bed and closed her eyes, breathing deeply and rhythmically, and just as the next pain came twenty minutes later, Gibby came through her bedroom door, eyes wide, breath short, looking at her with an excited smile on his face.

"How is it going, are you doing all right? Trying to relax and breathe," he asked in as calm a voice as he could. She nodded, though her eyes were closed and her whole body was straining with the pain that she felt. The contraction lasted a while, and then disappeared, and she leaned back against the pillows once more and tried to catch her breath as she opened her eyes and looked up at her best friend.

Gibby sat at the edge of the bed and held her hand in his. "All through with that one? Was it very difficult?" His eyes searched hers questioningly.

She sighed and closed her eyes a long moment and then looked up at him and nodded. "Yeah, that one is done. It's been about twenty minutes, I guess. They aren't terrible, but it does hurt pretty badly. If they're all like this, I might not do the drugs, but if they get worse, I'm definitely going to want some pain reliever."

He stood up and held his arms out open to her. "Well, there's just one place you're going to get that. We need to get you to the hospital." He told her as he grinned happily.

She swung her legs off of the bed and reached up to hug him, and he pulled her to her feet. "So, that's your hospital bag there, by the bedroom door?" he asked, looking over at the bag she had packed two weeks before.

She nodded and he walked over to her closet, pulling the doors open and then planting his hands on his hips. "Hmm… what to wear to give birth to a first child… something strong, something feminine, something comfortable and easy to remove. I know they're going to put you into one of those wretched hospital gowns, but at least you can look good going in. Let's see…" he flipped through the row of clothes hanging in her closet and finally pulled out a pull over sundress in a buttercream yellow.

"This is adorable. You'll look wonderful. Slip on sandals. You'll be all set." He stood behind her and helped her into the dress carefully, and then held her hand and walked with her as he carried her suitcase in the other hand. They made it to the front door just as Matthew pulled into the driveway.

She looked over at him as he bolted from his car toward her, just as she was coming out of the front door and she felt awash in relief to see him.

"Matthew!" she called out to him. He looked harried and in a full panic. Gibby stopped where they were and looked at the man rushing toward them. River Lea heard him hum thoughtfully, and she realized that they hadn't ever met before.

160

"Gibby, this is Matthew; he's the baby's father. Matthew, this is Gibby, my best friend." She made the quick introduction, and Gibby's eyes moved over him in swift appraisal.

"Well, Matthew, it's good to meet you. I think perhaps you had better help our young lady here to the car, and I'll take the bag. Let's get going, this little girl isn't going to wait for us to get there." He let go of River Lea's hand and walked over to Matthew's car. He waited by the trunk as Matthew helped River Lea to the passenger side door, and then into her seat. He looked steady, but not really calm.

He opened the trunk for Gibby, and Gibby put her bag into it and closed it, and the three of them rode off quickly to the hospital, all of them anxious to meet the little girl who was about to make her debut.

River Lea had another contraction just as they reached the hospital, and Matthew held her hand through it, looking desperate to do anything he could to make it better or help her in some way.

She powered through it, and when it subsided, she went in with both men and was taken to the maternity ward.

The nurses set her up in her delivery room, which was decorated in pastel colors and looked more like a comfortable bedroom than a hospital room. River Lea had another contraction, and both Gibby and Matthew stood on either side of her, helping her through it. As the contractions came at closer intervals, they became stronger and more painful, and River Lea had to get an epidural.

The nurses and doctor continued to check on her, and the closer she got to delivery, she noticed that they were becoming more concerned with the way that Charlie was positioned in her, and discussions of needing to do a possible C-section came up.

Both Gibby and Matthew were worried about her and the baby, staying strong for her while hoping that the baby would turn and she could have a natural delivery. Both of them remained at her side until the staff told Gibby that he would have to wait in the waiting room.

The doctor came to Matthew and River Lea and told them that the baby had not moved where he needed her to be for the delivery, and that it was looking as if they were going to have to prepare for a C-section. River Lea was afraid of going through any kind of surgical procedure, and she was concerned for both herself and the baby making it through all right. Matthew looked at her directly and held her hands tightly in his as the nursing team prepped her for the operation.

"I'm here, and I'm going to stay here with you. I'm not going anywhere. You're going to make it through this just fine. You're strong and young, and this little girl is just as strong as you are. She's going to make it through as well, and everything will be alright. We can do this. All three of us... we can do this," he told her convincingly.

She felt more sure of what they were about to go through as she listened to him. He kept his eyes on hers, and she told herself that if she just watched him, she could make it through the delivery. She wrapped her fingers tightly around his and found a strength in him that she was able to cling to.

Her contractions grew stronger and more frequent, and as she struggled through each one, she began to feel weaker and weaker, and though she tried not to worry, she saw concern and worry not only in Matthew's eyes, but also in the doctor's eyes, and she made herself a promise that no matter what they knew or thought, both she and Charlie were going to make it through the birth and come out of it healthy and strong.

Just as the medical team were about to get started on the Caesarean section, Charlie moved and turned, and the doctor smiled wide, breathing in relief as he and the nurses moved all of the surgical equipment away and positioned themselves for a natural childbirth.

Matthew and River Lea both looked at each other with a gasp and he hugged her tightly, both of them overwhelmed with happiness that there didn't need to be a C-section. The doctor looked at

River Lea seriously and spoke in a calm but firm voice.

"You've really been worn out going through everything you've gone through to get this far. You're going to need all of your strength to bring this baby into the world, so try to rest as much as you can between contractions, and do whatever it takes to reserve what little strength you have left. You're going to need it." He watched her eyes, making sure that she understood just what he was telling her, and she gave him a nod of comprehension.

Matthew held tightly to her hand, and over a long and arduous forty-five minutes of struggling and pushing, she finally gave birth to a little girl. She was completely exhausted, but there were tears of joy streaming down her face as the doctor told her that the baby was alright, and he let Matthew cut the umbilical cord.

The nurses cleaned the little girl up and handed her to Matthew, who stared at her as if he had never seen a baby before. River Lea could see that he fell

165

in love with his daughter the moment he saw her, and she felt a rush of bliss and utter happiness course through her.

He brought the baby to River Lea and held the baby up to her. The little one had mocha skin like River Lea's, and blue eyes like the sea. Her little cherub face was round and sweet, and River Lea was certain that she had never seen a cuter baby in her life. Matthew didn't hesitate in placing the baby in River Lea's arms, and as she held the little girl, looking at her in complete amazement, she knew she would always be glad that she had given such a precious gift to the man standing beside her.

Matthew stared down at them both and she saw a strange expression come over his face. He was blissfully happy, but there was something else that she saw as she looked up into his eyes. There was a sort of sadness hinting at the edges of him, and she could feel it, and she realized that he must be wishing that Amil was there to share in the joy of the birth of their daughter.

The nursing staff took the baby away and the doctor came to Matthew and River Lea, looking serious again. He spoke to them both at the same time, his gaze moving back and forth between them.

"This has been a very difficult and taxing birth. River Lea, you're going to need some rest, and you're going to need a lot more help and rest after you leave the hospital. Your recovery is going to take some time and it won't be easy. Matthew, I hope you'll be seeing to that." He looked then at Matthew, and Matthew nodded earnestly.

"She'll be well taken care of. I promise you that," he vowed. She looked up at Matthew gratefully, and gave him a smile, but as she did, she felt as if there was a black hole somewhere inside her that was pulling her in, and she couldn't hold on to the world around her any longer. She closed her eyes and drifted quietly and slowly away, falling into the deepest sleep she had ever known.

It felt like a long time before she finally opened her eyes again and looked around herself. She was in a strange room, in a strange bed, and it took her a moment to realize that she was still in the hospital. . She took a big breath and lifted her hands to her stomach to feel for Charlie, but she found her stomach empty and it felt bizarre to her to touch a place that had been so full of life, and was now only her own body again.

Matthew was sitting near her bed, and to his side was an empty bassinet. In his arms was a little bundle all wrapped up in blankets. He was smiling at the little girl in his arms, and River Lea realized that he hadn't heard her wake up. She watched him for a time, staring at his daughter, and she loved seeing it and feeling the happiness that it gave her to know that she had made it possible for him to have such a special gift.

After a long while, he looked up at her and noticed that she was awake and watching him. He grinned at her and she smiled back.

"How are you feeling?" he asked with concern in his voice and in his eyes.

She took a deep breath and moved her body only slightly before she knew that she was in a great deal of pain from the birth. "I'm pretty sore, actually," she said quietly. He reached for the call button and pressed it to alert the nurse to come in.

"She told me to call her when you woke up because she wants you to get up and walk around a little bit. I guess that's how they start to get your body back to normal again. We can ask her for some pain medication while she's in here." He didn't have to wait long to ask, as the nurse came into the room right away.

She helped River Lea up out of the bed and walked her to the bathroom and back to the bed again, and then she brought her some medication. She told River Lea that she needed rest more than anything, and made it clear to Matthew that he was going to have to help her quite a bit. His expression sober, Matthew accepted everything the nurse told him. He promised he would, and the nurse left them.

After they were alone again, he set the sleeping baby back into her bassinet and looked over at River Lea, lying there in the bed beside him.

"River, I wanted to talk with you about what's going to happen next with us. I know in the contract it was set that after the birth, I would be taking the baby home with me, and you would return to your home, paid of course, and that would be that." He sighed and gazed at her intently.

"Obviously everything has changed since we originally made our agreement. There is no one at my home to help me with the baby, as there ought to have been. I haven't found a suitable nanny yet, and you are in no condition to be home alone. You're going to need a lot of care and help to recover. I was also thinking that it would really be best for Charlie if she nurses. They say that giving a newborn breast milk is just about the best thing that you can do for them.

So…" he drew in a long and deep breath, looking at her hopefully, "I was thinking if you're okay with it, I'd like for you to come back to my house with little Charlie and I. I can help take care of you and get you back on your feet again, and you can nurse Charlie, and you and I can help each other take care of her until I can find a nanny."

River Lea blinked and stared at him. "I… I guess I thought that Gibby would be taking care of me, but I can see your points. I know it's going to be a long road to recovery for me, and I know you need the help with her… but, are you sure about this? Are you really sure? I'm a little hesitant to do it because I'm not sure I want to bond with her and then have to give her up.

I'm not sure it will be easy to walk away if I spend a lot of time with her in her first few weeks of life. Does that make sense?" She hoped that it did. She wasn't sure how bonding worked, but she had heard of it, and she didn't know if she could bond with another woman's baby or not, but it was a risk she was not keen on taking.

Matthew shook his head. "Well, you do need the help, and so do I, and I think it would only be for a few weeks. I really feel like it's the best for all of us if this is how we handle it. We'd all be taking care of each other, and I think that's just what we all need."

She pressed her lips together and looked from him to the clear little bassinet behind him, and the infant bundled up in soft pastel pink blankets. She thought of how much he had changed and how he had gone from wanting her to keep the baby to wanting to keep Charlie and give her a good home. She knew that he could probably figure out some of the baby care she would need, but she knew that no matter how dedicated he was, he would have a hard time on his own, especially in the first few weeks.

She also knew that she was going to need a lot of care and help herself, and while she knew that Gibby would be there for her no matter what for as long as she needed, she also didn't want to impose on him too much or take him too far out of his normal life routine.

What Matthew was suggesting sounded like the best possible plan, and she realized that he was right about it. It was the best idea for all of them. Sighing in resignation, she looked back at him and gave him a nod.

"All right, but just until you find a nanny. Then I'll go back to my world, and you and Charlie will be all settled in yours. Right?" she raised her eyebrows seeking agreement from him. He smiled and agreed with her, and it seemed set between them.

The nurse came back into the room not too long after that and helped River Lea learn how to nurse Charlie, and though Matthew had turned away at first to give them a little privacy, he soon was fascinated with it, and came back to River Lea's side to watch after she told him that it didn't bother her for him to be a part of it.

The connection that she felt with Charlie as the baby nursed from her was one she never expected to have. It was as if part of her own self was there in her arms, being nurtured by her body, and it felt

173

like a perfect circle to her. She loved the closeness, and the way that the little girl felt in her arms and smelled when she nuzzled her nose and lips close to the baby's face.

Gibby came back by the hospital a short while later, bringing with him a massive balloon bouquet, as well as a bouquet of flowers, and the cutest little raggedy teddy bear that River Lea had ever seen. He explained that every baby needs its own teddy bear, and after a long and dedicated search, he had finally found just the right one for little Charlie. Both River Lea and Matthew loved it.

He stayed with them and talked with them for a long while that afternoon, holding the baby and cradling her against his heart until she woke up and needed to nurse again, and then he hugged River Lea and Matthew both, congratulating Matthew, and leaving with a promise to call River Lea later.

It wasn't until Matthew went home late that night that River Lea called Gibby back to talk with him

174

about the plans that she and Matthew had agreed to.

"So, Gibby, there have been some changes in the plans that we made for recuperation. I hope you're not offended or anything. I mean, I don't think you will be, but I just wanted you to know that it's nothing at all personal," she began as she thought about how she would tell him the news.

"What changed? What's going on? Are you okay?" he asked, and she heard the genuine concern in his voice.

"Yes, I'm fine, thank you. Or… at least I will be. The birth really knocked me out, and the doctor said it's going to take some time to get me back up on my feet again, and that I will need some really good care and help, and I know that you were going to be the one to do that, but Matthew and I talked, and we were thinking of doing something else." Her voice was soft and gentle.

"Oh? What did the two of you come up with?" he asked curiously.

She bit at her lower lip for a moment and then answered him. "Well, it was actually his idea. He asked about me coming to stay at his house just for the first few weeks so that I have a place to heal and so I can nurse the baby. Breast milk is best, they say, and he doesn't have anyone there to help him with Charlie yet.

He is going to hire a nanny, but he hasn't had time, so it's just him taking care of her right now and that could prove to be a little more difficult than he's ready for. Not that I know that much more about taking care of a new baby, but I feel pretty sure that I know more than he does, and I know I'd be a big help to him. So…" she hesitated, "what do you think?"

Gibby was quiet, and she thought she heard him sigh a little. "What do I think? Well… I think it's a good idea, and I know you would certainly be a help to him and that little girl, but I am wondering if you might get attached to the baby and have a hard time leaving when you're done there, and I'm not sure how it would be for the two of you being around each other taking care of her together. Would that be weird for you? I mean, weirder than it already is?"

She tipped her head and gave his words some thought. "No, I don't feel like it would be too strange. I think I could do it. I think I could actually make a big difference there for her and for me. Or, I guess for all three of us. Anyway, I told him that I would do it, and I wanted to tell you about that."

"Okay, but if it gets weird at any point, or you just decide that you want to go home, you let me know and I'll be over there to take care of you. I know how much you don't want to be an imposition to me or to anyone else, but you aren't one, and I'm your best friend, and I want you to remember that. All right? So, if you change your mind, you just tell me. I'll be right over." He sounded resolute, and she smiled, thankful to have such a good friend.

"I really appreciate that, Gibby. I'm so lucky to have you. Thank you," she replied happily. "I do

177

think it's going to be okay, and also, it's just for a few weeks tops, so I'll be okay."

He seemed to accept that. "So how are you feeling anyway? When I left you looked like you were better, but it's seriously the most you've ever been through. I wanted to ask the doctor what in the world he'd done to you!"

"Oh no, the doctor is one who made this all happen as good as it possibly could have. I almost had to have a C-section, but then Charlie turned at the last minute, and I was able to do a natural delivery, but if it wasn't for the doctor, things might have been a whole lot worse. I know I looked bad, and it seems like it was bad, but truly it could have been so much worse," she told him earnestly.

Gibby sighed in relief. "I'm just glad that you're okay, and that the baby is okay." She detected a note of pride in his voice. "That's one cute kid. I was going to tell you that I think it's pretty incredible that Matthew decided to keep her name and still call her Charlotte like we have been. I thought he'd have given her another name altogether, but he kept it the same and that's pretty cool. He seems like a good guy."

"Yeah, well, think about it this way; until this last week, he wasn't even planning on taking her home, so he wouldn't have needed to come up with a different name, but I'm glad that he kept this one, too. You know how special it is to me." She smiled thinking of it.

They talked a while longer, and then she tried to stifle a yawn and he heard her do it, and told her that he better let her go so that she could get some rest. She agreed and got off of the phone. Within minutes of ending the call, she was fast asleep.

When she woke up, the nurse was there with Charlie and she was able to nurse the baby. She held the little girl in her arms and looked down at her sweet tiny face, and they gazed into each other's sea blue eyes, almost like a mirror. When River Lea had asked the nurse about Charlie's blue eyes, the nurse had told her that babies are often born with blue eyes and then shortly after the birth, the eyes turn another color, especially if they are dark. River Lea liked them blue, and told Charlie all about it.

She told her about her new life and her dad, and how it would be going home soon. She told her about the teddy bear that Gibby had brought for her, and how she was going to go home with Charlie for two or three weeks. She explained that it wasn't permanent, but that it was going to be nice for the two of them to have just a little more time together before River Lea had to tell her goodbye, and Charlie stared at her in wide eyed wonder, listening to every word from her with rapt attention.

The next day, the doctor told her that she could leave, and Matthew loaded River Lea and Charlie up in his car, along with a huge array of gifts from the hospital, and they all went to his home. River Lea hadn't known quite what to expect when she got there, but she didn't expect what he showed her at all.

He had made her own room for her, across the hall from his, and even though the nursery was set up, he had brought the bassinet into her new room so that she would have the baby nearby her to nurse and care for.

The bedroom was just as nice as Matthew's was, but it was a little smaller. *It was perfect for her*, River Lea thought, and she was relieved and happy to be there. He looked like the anxious and doting father, almost hovering in a way as he moved around the room getting everything set just so for the two girls. When they were both nestled into their respective beds, he stood just over the bassinet, looking down at his daughter, and he spoke to River Lea.

"I want you to know that you'll have all of the privacy that you want, but I will still be just across the hallway there, and if you need anything, you just let me know. I'm here to take care of you both, so don't forget that. Whatever I can do to make either of you more comfortable... whatever it might be, please let me know. Also, you have full run of the house and grounds, so if you want anything from the kitchen or the library, or if you want to go outside for some fresh air or a walk, or a swim... please feel free to do whatever you like. For the next couple of weeks, this is your home too." He gave her a nod and an encouraging smile and she smiled in return.

"I appreciate that so much. Thank you, Matthew. You're generosity and kindness are incredible," she answered him.

He looked sharp for a moment as if he had forgotten something, and he walked over to the wall of windows on the far side of the room and pulled all of the curtains open, and one of the glass doors, so that River Lea could see out.

She was amazed at the stunning view of the Pacific Ocean from her room, and as she saw it, she gasped with delight, and he grinned to see how happy it made her. He offered to close it so that she could sleep, and she asked him to leave it open for her so she could look out over it. He told her that when she was feeling up to it, there was a pathway from the house that led down to the private beach at the shoreline. She told him she would definitely be exploring that when she was up and around a little easier.

They gave each other a big smile, and he left the girls so that they could rest, but he was back in the room a short while later when the baby woke up. He'd brought in some of the baby clothes and diapers, and several other things from her nursery that he thought she might need, and River Lea was pleased to see just how hard Matthew was trying to make things good for them both.

He sat on the bed with River Lea and he changed Charlie's diaper and her clothes, and when the baby was settled once more, River Lea took her into her arms and nursed her until she fell asleep. Matthew had moved up to the pillows where River Lea was sitting up, and he nestled in beside her to be close to them both and be as much a part of it as he could. When the baby fell asleep, River Lea gave her to her father so that he could hold her, and he held her until he had fallen asleep too.

River Lea took the baby out of his arms and tucked her into her bassinet, and then she went back to her bed and laid down where she had been beside Matthew. It wasn't long after that that he turned toward her and slept beside her, his arm wrapped carefully around her waist. River Lea smiled to herself and let herself fall away into sweet dreams.

It didn't feel awkward to her to wake up in his arms. When she opened her eyes she found herself nestled against his chest, and she closed her eyes for a long moment, breathing in the scent of him and feeling the warmth of his skin against hers and the sturdiness of his arms around her. It felt so good to her, like she belonged there, and there could be no other place that she'd want to be. It occurred to her that she could definitely understand how little Charlie could fall asleep against him so easily when she was crying and he held her and rocked her.

When Matthew woke up, he found River Lea already awake, wrapped up in his arms, laying on his chest, and he worried for a moment that he might have done something that she didn't like or want, and she reassured him that everything was fine. He seemed glad to hear it, and when he was sure that she meant it, he held her closer, and they snuggled against one another a little more.

The baby didn't let them stay that way for too long; she let them both know that she needed them, and they were more than glad to be there for her. There was a pure sweetness to the care that they gave one another, and all three of them enjoyed it enormously.

Matthew only wound up spending the first night in his own room, and every night after that was spent in River Lea's room. They didn't really talk about it, other than at the beginning when he wanted to make sure that it was all right with her for him to be there, they just fell into it naturally. They were together most of the time in the house; Matthew had taken weeks off from work to be with his new daughter, and that meant that he was there with River Lea all of the time.

He made meals for them, he drew hot baths for her, and he took excellent care of both girls as they all adapted to the new changes of Charlie being home. River Lea and Matthew gave the baby her first bath, and after consulting a few of the baby books that he'd bought, they felt somewhat confident in getting it done without too many mistakes. The baby loved the warm water, and they loved the experience of helping each other take care of her.

River Lea didn't feel like a temporary addition to the family while she was there. She watched Matthew dressing his daughter after her bath, and as she did so, she realized that it felt like the three of them were a little family, rather than her just being there as a friend to help out in the first few weeks until a good nanny could be found to take her place.

She liked the feeling of being there, of being in the role that she had somehow found herself in, and she wouldn't let herself think of the imminent day that would come when she would leave. Instead, she focused on every single sweet little moment between the three of them, and loved all of those special and precious moments.

They took the baby in for her first appointment after her birth, and met the pediatrician together. River Lea wasn't sure if she should be there for it, or go with Matthew into the examination room, but he insisted, and she smiled and followed him in. She loved that the doctor talked with them both as if they were both the baby's parents and they each needed to know everything that she had to say to them about the newborn they were caring for together.

When they left the doctor's, River Lea suggested a walk, and since they already had the stroller, they went to the town center near his home and walked together in the warm sunshine, taking turns pushing the stroller, and talking with passersby who wanted to see the new baby. It felt like a family to her more and more, and from what she could see in Matthew, he was feeling the same thing. Though neither one of them mentioned it to the other, they both enjoyed it.

Night after night, he continued to stay in the room with her, and it became natural for the two of them to cuddle up together in the bed, holding each other as they fell asleep, and River Lea knew that eventually, when she left, she was going to miss that closeness, which made it all the more precious to enjoy while she had it.

She began to feel herself growing more attached to both Charlie and to Matthew, and at first she loved the feeling of it, but then as each day passed and she healed and felt better, and Matthew became more adept at caring for his daughter, she remembered that she was going to have to leave, and she knew that she was going to have to start distancing herself somewhat so that it wouldn't hurt as much when her time with them came to an end.

Matthew didn't talk about it or bring it up, but it was on River Lea's mind more and more often, and though she didn't mention it either, it felt to her like it was a shadow behind her, coming up closer to her; something she couldn't yet see and didn't need to deal with, but something that was coming nonetheless, and something she couldn't avoid.

Little by little, she made herself consciously put some distance between herself and the baby and Matthew. She did less with Charlie, letting Matthew do a little more of the work, and she began to do more things away from him while they were at the house, like doing the laundry on her own or going outside for a walk on her own while he was with the baby. She didn't distance herself from him at night, though, she knew she wasn't ready to start letting go of that closeness until she had to.

The sweet beautiful days of the three of them together became weeks, and somehow before they knew it, the weeks had become a month. They focused on one another, and River Lea was still distancing herself a little more often, and neither of them said anything about it until one morning when River Lea gave Matthew a sad sort of look and told him that perhaps it would be best if he gave the baby her bath on his own.

It caught him off guard, and he went to River Lea, his brown eyes steady on her blue ones, both of them looking troubled, and he frowned slightly. "You've been backing off some... I can feel it. You're... distancing yourself. River Lea, you don't have to do that. You can stay as long as you want to. I love having you here. We both do."

He reached his hand up to her cheek and his finger drifted across it gently as he spoke to her. She loved the feel of him touching her, as she always did; it had become a comfort to her, but she turned her face away from his hand and he watched her and let his hand fall back.

"I have to distance myself, Matthew; I'm leaving. I'm going to be leaving permanently. This is your home, and she is your daughter, and I was just supposed to be here for a few weeks and then I was going to go. It's been a month already, and it feels incredible to be here with you both, but this isn't my life.

My life is at home. I'm supposed to be going back to school soon, and me being all cocooned up here with you is like some kind of sweet, strange, magical dream, but it isn't going to last forever." She walked away from him and folded her arms across her chest, turning to face him again.

"You were supposed to be interviewing nannies to hire. Have you done that? Have you even talked to a single applicant since I've been here?" she asked, fairly certain that she already knew what the answer was.

He sighed and pressed his lips together into a tight line, pushing his hands down into his pants pockets. He gave his head a single shake. "No. I haven't really made the time to interview nannies. I guess… I guess I just got caught up in how perfect it is to have you here. I… I don't want this to change, but I know that's not what we agreed to."

191

He looked up at her and she swore her heart tried to melt right then just looking at him, but she steeled herself and lifted her chin as she spoke to him. "You're right, this does feel amazing, but this isn't reality. This isn't what it's going to be like forever. I'm leaving.

That's what the plan has been since we left the hospital. I was going to stay just long enough to heal and to help you with her until you could find a nanny, and you haven't even been looking. That's not fair to me, Matthew. You need to get on top of that and face up to your responsibility and find a nanny for her so I can leave. It's time for me get back to my life."

She hated saying it, and worse than that, she hated hearing herself say it, because it made it feel all the more real. She was going to leave them and she was going to go back to her life, and all of the things that she loved about Charlie and everything that she loved about Matthew, would be gone. Permanently.

Matthew drew in a long slow breath and hung his head, looking down at the floor for a minute. He didn't say anything, and she watched him, wondering what it was that he was thinking. At long last, he raised his head and looked at her and she saw disappointment in his eyes. "I'm sorry. I'll get started looking for a nanny right away."

He kept his gaze on her as he began to walk a few steps toward her."Just stay until I find a nanny, will you please? Would that be all right? You know I need you here, and Charlie needs you here as well. I'll look, just don't go until I find a nanny, please?" he asked, walking even closer to her. He didn't stop until he was directly in front of her, looking down into her face, his eyes locked on hers, and she could feel the warmth from the closeness of his body.

Her belly warmed as it often did when he was so near her, or cuddling her in her bed, and she made herself take a deep breath. She told herself that at least he was going to try to find someone to replace her. She gave him a nod. "Okay. I can do that. I will wait until you find a nanny, but you need to make that happen really soon, please. I can't..." she sighed and made herself say it, though she didn't want to, "I can't stay here with you two."

"I understand," he told her, his eyes deeply connected with hers. She felt the pull between the two of them and she turned her face away from his and walked toward the bedroom door.

She looked over her shoulder at him. "Thank you, Matthew. It's been wonderful to be here, and I've loved it, but it's definitely time for me to go." With those words spoken, she left the room and headed outside for some fresh air in the garden.

Once outside, she strolled through the garden for a few minutes, but then decided to head down to the beach to feel the sea on her feet. She pulled her cell phone out and called Gibby. They had been talking regularly still while she had been there, though not nearly as often as they normally did.

He answered his phone and sounded glad to hear from her. "There she is! How are things going on baby hill?"

She sighed and sank down into the warm golden sand, pushing her toes and feet deep into it until they disappeared. "Not too good, actually," she answered with a sigh.

"Uh oh. Trouble in paradise?" he asked cautiously. "What is it? What's going on?"

River Lea stared out at the distant horizon and thought about it before she answered him. "What's going on is that I feel like I've been here too long, and I feel like I'm getting too attached to the baby and maybe even a little to Matthew, and I'm sure it's just hormones, but that doesn't make it any easier."

He hummed a little, as if a light had come on in his head, and he had a better comprehension of what was going on with her. "I see. You're bonding with baby and baby daddy, and you know it can't last and you have a walk-out date coming up soon. That's it?"

"Yes. That's it exactly. It's getting harder to even think about leaving, but I'm going to have to leave at some point soon; I have school coming up, and I can't just stay here, I have to go. I have to get back to my life!" She covered her eyes with her hand and took a deep breath.

"Well, honey, all you have to do is let me know when you want me to come pick you up, and I'll be there. You know that. You're a phone call away from changing it all. I'm ready whenever you are," he told her bluntly. His voice was casual and matter of fact, but his words struck truth in her.

"I know that. I know it really is my choice when I leave, but I did promise Matthew that I would stay until he found a nanny, just to help him with Charlie." She sighed and her shoulders drooped some.

"Well, obviously he hasn't found one that he likes yet. Is he close? Does he have it down to a couple and he just needs to choose one, or what?" Gibby asked expectantly.

She shook her head, though she knew he couldn't see her, and she made a fist and mashed it into the sand. "No, he doesn't have it down to a couple; he hasn't even been looking for one! All this time that's gone by, he was supposed to be finding one, and he hasn't even started yet! I think he doesn't want me to leave. Well, actually, he told me that I don't have to leave, that I can stay here as long as I want to, and part of me does want to, but I can't do that! I have a life, and I have to get back to it, and he has a little girl, and he needs to focus on her. That's that. That's how it has to go."

Gibby hummed again. "It sounds like you're getting in much too deep, my dear. It sounds like you are far more attached than you ever should have gotten. It's time to go."

"I know that," she said quietly, feeling listless.

"So, help him find a nanny and call me, and I will come and get you. Set a timeline. Set some goals, and make it happen. Get out of there before you become too invested and get hurt. You're not where you are supposed to be. You're supposed to be at home getting ready for school. You're supposed to be living your own life. You've healed by now, I take it, and you're probably capable of being home on your own, so make that happen.

Every single day you spend there beyond today is just an indulgence and it's just a little more time that is going to make you feel the pain of leaving just a little bit sharper, so get out. I'm telling you this because I love you and I don't want to see you get hurt. Get out. Soon. Okay?" he said, as if that was the clearest directive ever spoken.

She picked up a handful of the soft sand and let it run through her fingers. "Okay. I know you're right. I'll make it happen and get out of here. Thank you, Gibby. I appreciate it so much. I love you, too. I don't know what I'd do without you."

He smiled and she could hear it in his voice as he spoke. "You're never going to have to find out what you'd do without me. So get back home, and we'll go forward with life. Okay? Dinner on the deck soon, yes?"

"Yes. That sounds perfect." She smiled and thanked him once more before ending the call.

She looked around at the beach and the sea before her, and felt the serenity of it seep into her and relax her. She loved being there, but it was definitely time to leave, and Gibby was right, she had to go before she got any more of her heart invested in Matthew and Charlie.

Chapter Six

Things remained the same for a couple more days, and then River Lea decided that she had to make some changes on her own. The first change was to move the bassinet out of her room and into the nursery. There was a top of the line baby monitor in the nursery, and she set up the monitor cameras and speakers in both her room and in Matthew's room.

He hadn't slept in his own bed since the first night she had come home from the hospital, and though they had gotten used to sleeping beside one another, she knew it was going to have to change right away if she was ever going to make herself leave. She showed him what she had done, and he didn't say anything at first, but his jaw clenched a little, and she noticed it. He turned away from her and nodded silently.

"I guess it must be time to get our girl into her own room," he said quietly.

"Well, I think she's still going to need us through the night, but at least this way she'll get used to being in the nursery. The monitor is there for us and for her, and the nursery is connected to your room, so you'll be able to hear her, anyway, and you're right there for her. She is just a little further away," River Lea explained.

He looked up at her then and the expression on his face hurt her heart. He seemed disappointed and perhaps even a little at a loss. "Both of you will be further away, I guess." His voice didn't hide his feelings.

River Lea turned her gaze from him and busied herself with gathering baby clothes and diapers. "So have you made any progress with the nanny search?" she asked as lightly as she could, wishing that he would tell her that he'd found one, while simultaneously wishing that she could stay and not ever have to leave. She pushed the thought from her mind and made herself focus on what she knew the best solution was. She made herself concentrate on the reality of their situation.

"I did contact some agencies, and they are sending a few nannies out for us to interview. They will be here tomorrow during the day. I thought it would be best to have them here while the baby is napping." His voice sounded hollow, and she continued to look away from him as she slowly folded Charlie's clothes.

"That's good," she said quietly. Then she turned slightly, but didn't look all the way up into his eyes. "You know, I don't need to be part of the interviewing process. That's something you could do without me," she told him in a gentle tone.

He walked toward her and stopped just behind her. She could feel the nearness of him, though he wasn't touching her. When he spoke, his voice was deep and soft in her ear, just over her shoulder, and she closed her eyes and tried to stop the familiar warmth that began to spread through her the way it always did when he was near.

"I want you to be part of it. You're the closest thing she has to a mother right now; you carried her for nine months, you brought her into the world, and I know she means a great deal to you. You have cared for her like she was your own since she was born. You should be there to help me choose the nanny who will take care of her when you..." he hesitated, and she knew he didn't want to say the words, "...when things change."

Biting at her lower lip, she finally sighed and nodded. He was right. She did want to be sure that her little Charlie had just the right person looking after her every day. "All right. I'll do the interviews with you. It's important to me to make sure that she's well taken care of. Thank you for being so thoughtful about that. It means a lot to me."

She could feel him watching her and she knew if she turned around, things between them would feel even warmer than they already did. Instead, she picked up the small pile of baby clothes that she had in her hand and walked out of her room and into the nursery where she put them away and took a deep breath, telling herself that she had no business feeling anything for Matthew like she was feeling. She could not allow herself to look at him the way that she was, or to want him as she did. She had to concentrate on getting out of his home and his life, and letting herself think about what it felt like to be in his arms was an indulgence that she couldn't afford.

River Lea took her time getting back to her room, and when she did return to it, he was gone. She frowned and felt a tightness in her chest as she walked over to the closet and pulled her suitcase out. She laid it on the bed and opened it up, staring into the emptiness of it, telling herself that she was doing exactly the right thing, and that it was far past time for her to go.

She packed her bag slowly, setting each piece of clothing into it carefully, wishing that she was already gone and that she didn't have to ever leave. She left a few articles of clothing out to wear the next day for the nanny interviews, but everything else she had was ready to go, so that when the nanny was hired, she leave.

When it was time for bed that night, she helped Matthew put the baby down, and tried to stop herself from thinking about how it would be to sleep alone in her bed that night. They stood over Charlie's crib and looked down at her, smiling and enjoying the closeness of each other as well as the moment they were sharing with her as she drifted slowly off to sleep.

River Lea could feel the need in her for Matthew to hold her, and it was so strong that it was almost tangible. She made herself turn her back to him and walk away from the crib, until she had reached the doorway of the nursery. She turned then and looked over her shoulder at him. He was watching her with a fiery and intense gaze.

"Have a good night, Matthew," she said softly, and he responded quietly to her.

"You as well." It was all he said, and she turned away from him and made herself walk to her room.

She closed her bedroom door behind her, and went to her bed, hating getting into it alone. It felt cold and somehow it felt wrong; like everything that should be there was missing. She tried to ignore it as she closed her eyes and willed herself to sleep. She told herself that she had slept alone most of her life, and that this was no different, and it was definitely no time to wish for Matthew to be holding her in her bed.

It took a long while, and some serious effort on her part as she made herself think of everything else but him, but eventually she did finally fall asleep. He might not have come to her in person, but he did come to her in his dreams, and she found some comfort in his presence there, until the morning light woke her and she laid her hand on the empty pillow beside her, swallowing the lump in her throat and blinking back unwanted tears. She knew then that it was going to be one of the hardest things she had ever done, when the time came to walk out of his house and his life, and away from Charlotte, and never look back again.

She showered and dressed, and went to the nursery. Matthew was standing at the window with the baby, holding her and rubbing her back. When River Lea came in, he turned to face her, and she could see something very much like relief wash over him. He smiled at her and she took the baby from him, kissing the little girl and talking to her softly.

He watched her for a long minute before he spoke. "How did you sleep?" he asked, his eyes steady on her.

She turned from him slightly and focused her attention on the baby. She hadn't slept too well at all, but she didn't want to tell him that. "I slept okay. How about you?" she returned the question, expecting him to say something similar in answer to her.

He sighed a little. "I didn't sleep too well. It's… strange… sleeping without you. I missed being beside you. I guess I got too used to that too fast."

She couldn't respond to him, and it only took a moment for him to realize that there was an awkward air between them. He shrugged and looked out of the window. "I'm sorry. I guess I shouldn't have said that. I can be too honest, sometimes. I'm sure it's just because it's different. I'll get used to it." He tried to sound lighthearted, and she felt a little sorry for them both. The change wasn't easy.

Shortly after Charlie went down for her nap that day, the first of three nannies showed up to be interviewed. The first one was an older lady who had been widowed. She seemed nice, though she made it clear that she was adamant about adhering to rules and regulations.

The second nanny was in her early twenties, and explained that she was only working as a nanny long enough to get through school. She was going to the same college that River Lea was going to, and they discovered that they knew some of the same people, though the people that she knew were people who River Lea would not have been friends with.

The third lady was a single mother with two of her own children, and she stated that she wanted to have the three of them living in the home with Matthew and Charlie, and she would take care of all of them together.

Matthew and River Lea thanked each one of them in turn for coming, and after they left, Matthew and River Lea looked at one another and sighed heavily.

"I think this might take a little longer than we anticipated," he said in a low tone.

River Lea looked at him thoughtfully. "Well, that first one seemed all right, I think. A little strict, perhaps…" she said, her voice trailing off. She wasn't totally sold on the woman, however, and she could see that Matthew wasn't either.

"I think she'd be too strict. I don't want someone who might be too harsh with Charlie." He sighed in resignation. He rubbed is hands over his face and then folded them together beneath his chin. "I guess we'll have another agency send some more over as soon as they can."

River Lea nodded and stood up to leave, but Matthew stood up swiftly and reached for her arm before she could step away from him. He closed his fingers gently around it, and she turned and looked up at him.

His eyes were locked on her, and she felt the rising heat between them as he stood so near her. "You'll stay until we find one... won't you?" he asked worriedly, and then he leaned a little closer to her and she lost her breath as he spoke. "Don't leave yet... please River Lea..." His eyes were wistful, and she swallowed hard, trying not to let herself feel everything that was beginning to rush through her just then.

"I'll stay until you find one, but it has to happen fast. I have to go soon," she answered him, and then she turned and he let her arm go, and she walked away, leaving him in the drawing room as she headed up to the nursery.

All the way up to the second floor, she tried to steady her breathing and tell herself that everything she was feeling was hormones, and that she had no business at all wanting him, wanting to be in his arms or feel him so close to her, or even wanting anything more than that from him. She forced herself to think of school, and of her house, and of Gibby, and of the life that was waiting just around the corner for her. The life that was really and truly hers, and the life where she belonged.

That night as they tucked little Charlotte into her crib, he looked down at his daughter and spoke quietly to River Lea without looking at her.

"I contacted two more agencies today. They are sending out some more nannies to interview in about three days." She could hear that he didn't like saying it at all.

"Three days? They couldn't send them any sooner?" she asked in surprise. She felt in her heart that he was stalling, and that there must certainly have been some place that could have sent some nannies out to them sooner than that.

He frowned and then turned to face her, looking into her eyes. "You don't have to go, River Lea. I know you feel like you do… I know you have your home and everything… but, you don't live that far from here. Your place is only half an hour away. You could stay here and go to school from here. You could… just… stay," he said quietly, looking into her eyes as she stood beside him.

She wanted to tell him no, to tell him that she had to go before she wouldn't be able to make herself let him go, but she couldn't speak. Her voice was gone, and her heart was pulling her towards all that she wanted—the man standing right before her.

He reached his hand up to caress the side of her cheek, and she felt the heat between them grow so hot it almost took her breath away. She closed her eyes and parted her lips, trying to take in a breath. Before she could, she felt both of his hands on her face, and an instant later, his mouth was on hers, soft, hungry, persistent.

Her heart tried to beat itself out of her chest as she gasped, drawing in a deep breath and closing her hands over his. She didn't try to move his hands; instead, she let her fingers slide down his arms until she reached his waist, where she wound her arms around him and he kissed her even more adamantly.

Matthew's fingers moved over her cheeks and down to her neck. His tongue found hers and as they tasted one another, she felt herself melting into him. It was unlike anything she had ever known before, and the more they kissed, the hotter everything between them became. Their breath grew shallower as the burning fires between them consumed all of their oxygen, and their need for one another became urgent.

She couldn't hold in the soft moan that escaped her as his arms closed firmly behind her, pulling her to him, and at the sound of it, he gasped and moved his mouth to her neck, kissing her there and whispering her name like a prayer.

River Lea moved her hands up his back and as his mouth found hers again, she let the last of her inhibitions go, kissing him with all of the desire

213

she felt inside for him. It overwhelmed them both, and he took her face in his hands and stared hard into her eyes.

"River Lea… I need you. I need all of you, please… make love with me now." His voice was hoarse and his eyes had never been more intense.

She closed her eyes and nodded her head, knowing that she probably shouldn't do it, and not caring at all that there would probably be consequences to have to face later. She looked up at him and in answer to his plea, she kissed him passionately. "I want you, too, Matthew, so badly."

He took her by the hand and walked with her to his bed, stopping only when they had reached the side of it. Slowly, in between the hungered kissing, they peeled each other's clothes off, and he laid her back in his bed, moving above her as he kissed her.

Flames seemed to burn through every part of her body as their bodies pressed against one another. She felt his erection against her thigh and it made her lose her breath, aching for him even more. She moved her fingers over the hardened curves of his muscles, feeling them ripple and tense beneath her touch.

Matthew's hands canvassed her body, cupping her breasts, sliding over her waist, and gliding slowly down the length of her leg. His fingers squeezed her flesh firmly as he touched her, and she held tighter to him in response.

His mouth found hers again and he kissed her in fiery desperation, sucking and biting at her lips and drawing her tongue into his own mouth. He pressed his hard desire against her body and began to move lightly, making her arch her back and wish that he was inside of her. The teasing feel of him against her was almost more than she could take.

He looked down at her, his eyes locked on hers, and he whispered thickly, "It has been so difficult to hold this back from you. I've wanted this with you so badly; I can hardly believe that I'm awake and this isn't just another incredible dream."

"I want you too…" she answered him, "…and I never thought this would happen. I wouldn't let myself think of it, because I wanted it so much."

An almost animal groan sounded from the center of his chest and he slid his hand to her knee, opening her completely to him. She couldn't breathe as she held tightly to him, feeling him as he entered her for the first time, pushing himself into her slowly and carefully, deeply until he filled all of her, and she cried out softly from the intense pleasure that took over every part of her.

They began to move together as one, and in their rhythm, she felt a connection with him that she had never felt with anyone before; more than the searing flames that were consuming them, her heart burned just as hotly as her body did with his, and she could feel herself getting lost and found in him.

The intense ecstasy that coursed through all of her with every orgasm that she felt made her believe that it could not get any hotter with him, that she could not feel any more passion than she did with him, but as each new orgasm came, she realized that there was no limit to how incredible it could be between them.

Sweat beaded on their skin and they held each other tightly as they twisted and turned in their love wresting, kissing and touching everywhere that they could, until at last Matthew could hold himself back no longer, and he thrust himself into the furthest depths of her, crying out her name loudly as he came, flooding her with all of his passion.

When he was spent, and both of them were barely breathing, he rested himself on her, kissing her for a long moment before he laid beside her and drew her to his chest, holding her there, pressing his lips to her forehead, and again to her mouth.

Their panting began to slow and as their bodies calmed, he held her, entwining his fingers with hers. They did not speak, but their love language spoke volumes for them. They ran their fingers lightly over each other's skin, they kissed softly, and they sighed in complete satisfaction, resting only until their touching and kissing began to stoke the fires of desire between them again, and a short while later, he was hard for her once more, entering her with more hunger than before, and more need, and they made love again.

After the third coupling between them that night, they both fell asleep in each other's arms, exhausted and blissful, and they stayed that way until the early morning hours when River Lea began to think about how she was supposed to be leaving, and how she had promised herself that she would not become more attached to either Matthew or Charlie, and yet there she was, in her new lover's arms, feeling as if she never wanted to leave them.

Reality crept its cold icy fingers around her heart, and she knew that she had no choice. She knew that if they awoke together and he made love with her again, she wasn't going to leave, and nothing would be what it was supposed to be.

 She knew she couldn't take that chance. She knew that she couldn't risk not being able to leave, and it was that, and only that, which made her kiss him on his mouth once more as he slept, before she slipped silently from the bed, gathered her clothes and disappeared from his room, going to her own.

She showered and tried to force herself not to cry. She dressed in silence, and texted Gibby, asking him to come pick her up, and giving him the address. She fixed her hair and makeup a little, and then took her suitcase down the stairs to the main floor.

She had wanted to say goodbye to Charlie, but she knew she couldn't do it and still make herself leave. Walking away from the two people upstairs was the hardest thing she had ever done. When she saw Gibby's headlights in the predawn darkness as he drove up the driveway, she went outside and closed the door behind her, tears streaming down her face, and she was grateful to him for not saying a word to her as he helped her put her things in his car, and drove her away from Matthew Chase's house, from Matthew, and from the precious baby girl she had carried for him.

Gibby dropped her off at her home just as the sun was beginning to slip over the golden hills, coloring all of the world in light. He walked with her to her door, hugged her tight, and told her to call him if she needed anything. She only nodded in response and then went into her home and closed the door behind her.

It was freeing to be in her own home. She felt as if she could breathe, as if she could leave the whole world outside and find no safer, more comforting place to be. No other place that was as much a sanctuary, where she could be without emotional turmoil and chaos churning in her. The peace she felt allowed the tension in her to dissolve, and in its place there was nothing but exhaustion.

She made her way to her bed, and there she slept for the better part of the day, not rising from her bed until it was late afternoon. She wondered if she would hear from Matthew, and how he would feel and what he would think when he awoke alone. There was no message or contact from him on her phone, and the plastic box laid there on her bedside table staring back at her lifeless, like a black hole, with no connection to Matthew and Charlie; nothing at all.

River Lea left the phone and went to the kitchen to make herself something to eat. She forced herself to concentrate on every small detail of the process, telling herself that it was how her life was supposed to be, and that things were finally as they should have been the day after she had the baby.

She checked her phone to see if there was any message or call or any kind of contact from him whatsoever, but there was nothing all that day, and all that night. She cried a few times, missing both of them, wishing that she hadn't left, wishing that she had left much sooner, wishing that he was with her in her bed or that she was with him in his, wishing that she could hold Charlie close to her heart as she had so many times, wishing she could smell that sweet baby smell and look into the little girl's beautiful blue eyes.

With each breakdown, the loss seemed to grow, and she promised herself that it was just hormones and she was going through an adjustment period, and that at some point she would come out of it and be all right. She showered. She walked on the beach.

She double checked all of her registration and classes for school. She made smoothies and then made more smoothies to freeze for later. She tried to read one of her favorite books. She tried to focus on playing a video game. Nothing could distract her mind, her thoughts, or her heart from who she truly missed and wanted to be with.

The following morning when she awoke, there was an email from her bank, telling her that a deposit had been made into her account electronically. She looked at the sum of her account balance and knew that Matthew had paid her for her job in carrying and delivering Charlie. It was over. The contract was done, and there was nothing more to be done or said or had between the three of them ever again.

River Lea could not stop the tears that flowed from her over the finality of it all. Both Charlie and

Matthew had overtaken so much of her heart that she felt that almost none of it that was left was actually hers. She wept bitterly on and off at intervals for a few days, until she finally convinced herself that the tears were never going to dry, and the pain was never going to stop, so she might as well focus on anything else.

Luckily for her, Gibby showed up to check on her, and he made it his mission to cheer her up and remind her how sweet and wonderful her life had been before the pregnancy. It was only with him that she found some reprieve from the pain in her heart, though it didn't completely heal her.

He came around to see her often, and a few times he invited her out with himself and Brad to have fun on the beach or in town, giving her a temporary break from everything going on in her heart and her head.

School began shortly after that, and she buried herself in her classes and in her homework to a level that she never had before, hoping to find some kind of solace.

It seemed like much longer, but according to the calendar, three weeks had passed since the day she had left Matthew alone in his bed, when her phone rang. She had stopped looking at it constantly, hoping to hear from him, all the while knowing that she wouldn't.

She answered it casually, without looking to see who it was, as she studied a diagram in one of her textbooks.

"Hello?" she asked lightly.

The voice she heard made her heart stop. "River Lea? It's Matthew."

Everything in her froze and her eyes widened as she tried to remember how to breathe.
"...Matthew?" she asked in barely more than a whisper.

"I'm sorry... about everything. I'm... I hope you're doing okay." He was struggling with nearly everything he was trying to say.

She had no idea how to respond to him. It took her a long minute to compose herself enough to speak.

"What's wrong? Why are you calling? Is it Charlie? Is she okay?"

She had told herself so many times that he wanted nothing more from her, that she believed it, and the only reason that she could conceive of why he might be calling her was for the baby. Fear began to grip her as she wondered what could have happened that would make him need to contact her and she held her breath, waiting for his answer.

"It does have to do with Charlotte. It's Amil... actually. She has decided that she wants custody of the baby." His voice had a gravelly tone, as if he had to choke the words out and make himself speak them aloud.

River Lea's mouth fell open and she lost her breath all at once. It was impossible. "What? What do you mean she wants custody? What on earth is going on?"

As far as she knew, Amil wanted nothing at all to do with Matthew, or with her daughter, and that had been the end of it. She couldn't begin to

225

imagine what might have changed the woman's mind, or even more than that, why Matthew would be calling her about it.

"Can I come and see you please, to talk about this?" he asked with a miserable sigh. As soon as she heard it, she knew that he needed her, and she felt resolute in helping him.

"Yes, of course. Please come by. I'm here all afternoon," she answered him. He told her that he would be there within the hour, and she ended the call with her mind going a million miles an hour. She had no idea what she could possibly do to help him, but at the very least, she knew she could be a support system for him. There had to be some way for her to help make it right for him and for her little Charlotte.

She put her school books and computer away, and made some lemonade for them. Half an hour later, he was standing at her door, and when she opened it and saw him, she was awash in a wave of relief to see him. She hadn't realized quite how much she had missed him until she launched herself at him and wrapped her arms around him tightly, breathing him in and holding him against her.

He held her just as tightly and neither one of them wanted to let go. "God, I missed you so much. I didn't think I would miss you this much, but... oh, it feels so good to hold you," he whispered, and she could only swallow her tears and manage to whisper, "Me too." into his ear.

It was minutes before she finally let him go and walked into the house with him; her hand holding his, not wanting to let him go. They walked out to the deck together and sat in the lounge chairs just as they had the first night he came over to eat dinner with her. She smiled at the memory and then looked at him as she handed him a glass of iced lemonade.

"What's going on?" she asked, trying to keep the worry in her heart at bay.

He took a long drink from the glass of lemonade, and then set it on the table beside him and sighed heavily, raking his hand through the brown waves of his hair.

"It's Amil. She had a lawyer contact me today to tell me that she wants custody of the baby." He shook his head and closed his eyes as if he couldn't quite make himself believe it.

"Where is the baby?" she asked, wishing he had brought Charlie with him so she could see her. "I miss her so much. I can't even tell you… it's so hard to be away from her, and from you."

He looked up at her. "She's at home with the new nanny. I found one that seems pretty good. She's been doing well with Charlie, and Charlie seems to like her."

River Lea shifted her thoughts back to Amil and the strange situation that Matthew had found himself in. "Well, isn't it a good thing, I guess, if she wants to be a part of her own daughter's life? Don't you feel like that would be a good thing, even if you two aren't together anymore?"

He pressed his lips together into a tight thin line and shook his head. "No, not really." Clasping his hands together in front of him, he drew in a deep breath and looked intently at River Lea.

"There's a lot you don't know about. I told you that our marriage was cold for the last couple of years, and that it was my idea to have a baby so that we could try to find that spark again, and she agreed to it. Well, that's partly true, but partly not. Our marriage bed was cold, but her bed wasn't." He grimaced and looked nauseous as he spoke.

"I have a competitor in the business world, and he's not a good man. He's constantly battling me in every arena he can find to battle me in. It began in our college years when we were at the same college. He couldn't keep up with my grades and accomplishments, and he did everything he could to try to surpass my successes—even going so far as cheating. He almost got expelled for it.

We graduated and entered the business world and he competed with me for jobs. I got the ones he wanted. I did well, and I started my own business.

He started his own business in the same field. Always competing. He began to compete in charity work, which actually works out better for the charities because they wind up making more money.

He competes in community service and events... in growth and innovation... in every aspect. He's always competing. I found Amil and got married to her, and I guess that was more than he was willing to take." He rubbed his hand over his forehead and paused as he took another drink from his lemonade and set the glass back down.

He looked at the moisture on his fingers from the condensation on the glass and then rubbed his hands together before looking back up at River Lea.

"I didn't know it, but he decided to go after Amil so that he could have her for himself. She knew full well about all the competition from him, and I guess maybe she enjoyed having two powerful men both wanting her, but she began to have an affair with him. I suspected it, but I didn't catch her at it for a long time.

She had lost total interest in being with me, and she was a passionate woman; I knew she had to be fulfilling her needs somewhere with someone else, though I didn't know who until I came home from work early one day and found her screwing him outside by the hot tub." He looked away from River Lea for a moment and the profound disgust on his face conveyed to her exactly how he felt about what he had seen.

She didn't say anything, but she felt her own bile begin to rise in her throat at the thought of what she was hearing. It was beyond anything she could imagine that Amil could have betrayed him and cheated on him the way that she did.

He continued. "When I caught them there together, he just laughed at me and told me that he had been sleeping with my wife for over a year and a half, and that he was so good at it that she wanted him in my own house. He said our marriage was a joke, and that she wanted him more than she wanted me.

So, I told her that she could have him, and I kicked her out right then. She went with him. She and I met once afterward to talk about how we were going to handle everything, and by that time, you were pretty far along in your pregnancy. She said he didn't want the baby, and to be honest, that she didn't want it either. She told me to just keep it, and that she wanted all of her things. Well… the phone call I got today was quite a surprise. She has changed her mind about all of it."

River Lea frowned. "What do you mean? She wants the baby now? The other guy wants the baby too? What does she want?"

Matthew closed his eyes as if it was almost too much to bear, and he shook his head slowly before opening his eyes once more and looking directly at her. "I don't know who she has been talking to or why she changed her mind, but because of the divorce we're going through right now, she has decided that she wants everything. She wants the baby because it's worth money to her in the form of child support. She wants the house. She wants all my real estate property. She wants all of the money that I have currently, as well as all the money I will make for the foreseeable future. She wants everything."

He groaned and leaned back in the chair, covering his eyes with his hand again. River Lea just stared at him.

"You've got to be kidding." She couldn't begin to wrap her mind around it.

"Oh no... no. I'm not kidding. That's all straight out of her attorney's mouth. He's promising me that they will get everything they are asking for. Of course, my team of attorneys is guaranteeing me the exact opposite, but that doesn't make it any less of a nightmare." He let out a long, slow sigh and looked at her again. His eyes looked tired, and she could see that he hadn't been sleeping. Her heart went out to him and she looked at him imploringly.

"What can I do to make this better for you?" she asked with little hope. "How can I help you through this?"

He sat up again and rubbed his fingers against his temples. "I'm not exactly sure. I think more than anything, I wanted you to know because you carried Charlie, you gave birth to her, you cared for her the first several weeks of her life, and you are the closest thing she has to a mother. Who knows, maybe my lawyers will want you to testify that you were there doing all of that when her real mother was off sleeping with another man. Maybe... maybe I just need the support of someone I trust to see me through this."

She stood up from her seat and moved over to sit beside him, taking his hand in hers and looking into his eyes. "I can definitely be a strong supporter for you, and if I can help in court at all, I will be glad to do it, although I'm not sure how much weight I could bring to it. I will do it if you need it, but in the meantime, I am here for you, and I'm here for little Charlie. You are not alone in this."

He looked for a moment as if a whole mountain had been lifted from his shoulders, and he breathed a visible sigh of relief. "I can't tell you how much that means to me," he said quietly, and he wrapped his arms around her and held her, and she held him back.

It wasn't a passionate embrace, but it was filled with love and friendship, and she knew that he needed that more than anything else just then, and she was glad to be able to give that to him. It felt to her as if everything that had been feeling so off and so wrong to her since she had left him in his bed, was much closer to being made right again, and that gave her enormous peace of mind and happiness.

He stayed a little while longer and they walked on the beach together, and he told her about the changes that had already happened with Charlie. He showed her photos on his phone, and they talked about everything except Amil and her unbelievable divorce requests.

When he left, River Lea walked him to the front door of the house and he hugged her tightly, holding her to his chest. He kissed her cheek softly, and though he hesitated a moment and she wondered if he would kiss her lips, he didn't. He smiled at her gratefully and thanked her, and then went to his car.

She watched him drive away and it felt to her as if her whole heart had gone with him down the road and around the bend, disappearing with him when he was gone. She wished that somehow things could be different between them, and that they could be together. There were feelings in her heart that she hadn't ever felt before, and by the sheer magnitude of them and their strength, she knew that she was falling for him, and she knew that it was the last thing in the world that should happen.

She walked away from the door reminding herself that she needed to focus on school and her upcoming career. She needed to focus on herself, and she told herself that she could help him if it became possible, but she could not allow herself to want him as she had.

Confusion began to tie her mind in knots, and her heart right along with it, and she picked up the phone to call the only person she knew who might be able to help her think through it. Gibby heard the tangle of emotion in her voice and he told her he would be right over.

Fifteen minutes later, he was sitting on her back deck with his own glass of lemonade. "Well? What is it that's bugging you, my dear?" he asked casually, though his eyes remained steady on her as if he knew it was much more than a casual situation and was merely trying to keep things light.

She sighed and frowned, looking at him in consternation. "It's a pretty big mess. I guess Matthew's wife left him for another man. Some guy who has been in competition with him since college and who has been after just about everything of his since then. The guy finally managed to get Matthew's wife, and he caught them having sex at his house."

Gibby's mouth fell open. "Shut up… really? That's horrible! What a little slut!" he snapped and furrowed his brow.

"Well, I guess Matthew threw her out then, and when she left she said she didn't want anything, but now that they are in the middle of their divorce, she's gone and changed her mind and she wants everything; all his money, his house, his properties, his business, alimony, and she wants custody of the baby just so she can have child support! She's trying to take him to the cleaners, and he's going to have to go to court to fight it all!" She growled in aggravation and Gibby shook his head.

"Wow! What a piece of work she must be! That's terrible!" He looked astounded at the sheer audacity of it. "I hope she doesn't get Charlotte… I can't imagine anyone like her with the baby."

A deep maternal instinct burned in River Lea. "Oh, she's not going to get her hands on Charlie if there's anything at all that I can do about it. She might not be my baby genetically, but in every other way, she is mine, and I will help Matthew fight for her tooth and nail.

That crazy woman has no business with our little girl. None at all. She's the last person who should be around her; I don't care if she's the biological mother. She's a terrible person and she can't have Charlie, and that's all there is to it."

Gibby shook his head. "Well, you and Matthew can try to fight it. I wish you two all the luck, but I'm going to say this as well; this divorce and this woman are each his own problems to handle. Charlie might feel like your baby, but she isn't your baby; she does belong to that cow of a woman, and there's nothing you can do about that.

You might also want to watch how you try to help him in court, in case that turns around and bites you back and you wind up hurting him in court because you went to the house with him and stayed there when it wasn't supposed to be like that in the contract.

I'm not saying you can't support him and be there for him, or even that you should totally stay away from court, but I think you should remember that these are his problems, and you are not part of them in any way, shape, or form right now. Don't stir up trouble where there isn't any trouble… right? Do you know what I mean?" he asked her pointedly.

She saw the serious look in his eyes and she knew that he meant business, and she knew that he wasn't wrong about anything that he had said.

"I do know what you mean. I just… I feel so strongly about it and I want to help, but at the same time, I know you're right. That could easily backfire. I hadn't thought about what it might look like to someone on the outside in regards to me staying there after the baby was born." She frowned slightly.

Gibby leaned forward and put his arms on his knees, looking her straight in the eye. "Can I tell you what it looks like to someone on the inside in regards to your staying there so long after the baby was born?"

She blinked and her heart began to pound. "What…? What does it look like?" she asked just above a whisper.

"It looks from the inside like you started to fall for him. It looks like you think about him all the time, and like you miss him like crazy since you left him. It looks like a whole lot more than taking care of a baby happened up at the big old house while you were staying there, and it looks like you're trying to keep it under wraps, and talk yourself out of it, and try to convince yourself that you don't have the feelings for him that are so obvious to others of us." He kept his eyes locked on hers.

"That's what it looks like to someone on the inside, so to anyone on the outside, it will probably look worse. I'm just saying that that's something you should consider before you go blazing to the courts on a warpath, ready to take that baby girl from her biological mother. You might do more harm than good." He leaned back and watched her quietly, sipping his lemonade.

She stared at him in disbelief and then blinked and glanced away from him for a long moment. "All of that... is all of it that obvious?" she asked in an amazed whisper.

He nodded and rolled his eyes dramatically. "Sooo obvious."

She cringed a little and looked back at him. "Sorry. I thought I was doing much better than that about it."

He shook his head. "No. You aren't. Now, I don't know how much of it is hormones, and how much of it might actually be real emotion or even love, but I can tell you this. The truest test of love is time. If you can hold off and take your time with him, and all the things happening between you two, no matter how court goes, no matter how his divorce goes, no matter how custody of Charlotte goes… if you can be friends with him during all of that and still have the emotion there after a good amount of time has passed between the two of you, then you could start to think about serious things with him.

But in the meantime, if I was you, I'd chalk it up to a hot time in the hay, and leave it alone. Don't push for anything with him, especially right now. He's got a full plate, and there's no room for a new romance to grow in an environment like that. You'll strangle it if you try to push too much right now. Also, you don't want to hand any kind of helpful trouble to his ex-wife's attorney, and you two getting hot and heavy will do nothing but cause problems for him in court, so that has to stop pronto."

She sighed and leaned back in her chair, looking out at the ocean. "I can't stand how complicated this is. I was just going to have the baby, make the money, and get myself back to school. Now look at this mess."

He shrugged. "Hey, we can't help who we love or want… things just work out that way sometimes and there's not really any way around it. Just think about what I said and take your time. You aren't in a rush anyway. Nothing needs to be rushed. Just… get to know him and be friends and when this whole nasty legal mess blows over, then see where the two of you are at that point. If you're lucky, maybe good things will happen for the two of you. If not, well, you had a good time. Right?"

He looked over at her pointedly and she smiled and gave him a nod. "Yeah, I guess so. You know, your logical method of thinking is always such a big help to me in putting things into perspective. I tend to over think everything, and it always winds me up in trouble. Thanks for giving me a different way to look at it. I knew I could count on you to do that for me."

She gave him a smile and he reached his hand over to hold hers and give it a soft squeeze. "No problem. That's what friends arc for." He smiled back at her and they looked out onto the beach and surf together.

THE FINAL CHAPTER

Matthew and River Lea shared some texts over the following days and weeks; mostly they were photographs of Charlie, and updates on how things were going. There was nothing at all romantic in them, though there was deep emotion, and it felt to her as if the romantic feelings she had were shared by him, and were always right on the edge of all the conversations they had.

He called her two weeks after he had come to her home to see her. She was surprised to see that it was him calling her, and at first she was elated that he was reaching out to her, but that was followed immediately by a feeling of dread that she could not overcome, so worried was she about why he might be calling.

"Hello, Matthew?" she asked as she answered.

"Hi," he said with a heavy tone. She knew then that it wasn't going to be a pleasant call.

"Oh no… what's wrong?" she asked worriedly.

He sighed. "Can you come by the house? There has been a change in things, and I was going to just talk with you about it, but I know that you miss Charlotte and you'd love to see her, so I thought you could come by here and visit her, and we can talk. What do you think? Would you want to do that?" he asked with the slightest bit of hope in his voice.

She thought her heart might explode from all of the excitement that she felt. "Yes! My goodness yes, of course! I have some free time this afternoon if that works. I can come right over, or be there whenever you need me."

She hadn't seen the baby since the night she had put her to bed and she and Matthew had made love. She'd left before dawn that morning, and it had felt like she'd left part of her heart and soul behind her in the crib in the nursery. She was aching to see Charlie and hold her.

"We'll be here all day. Please come anytime you want to. Neither of us can wait to see you." She heard a small smile in his voice, and it made her heart glad to know that she could at least give him some slight happiness during such a dark time.

She told him that she would be right over and she hung up the phone. She changed her clothes and wore a pretty sundress with sandals, fixed her hair and makeup so that she looked as good as she felt, and then she got into her car and drove to Matthew's house.

She was so excited to see them both, especially the baby, that she was practically giddy all the way there, and it just grew as she pulled up to his house and parked her car there. He opened the door for her and wrapped his arms around her the moment he saw her, burying his face in her neck and hair, breathing her in, and holding her tight against him.

"God I've missed you." He spoke nearly in a whisper. She felt everything in her begin to move swiftly and all of it heated up just as it always did when she was around him. She remembered

Gibby's warning, and she made herself take a long slow breath as she stepped back out of Matthew's embrace.

"I've missed you too. It's so good to see you." She gave him a warm smile, and he stepped back a little from her and turned toward the living room.

"Someone else has been missing you, too," he said as he tipped his head toward the sound of a baby laughing and giggling.

Her eyes grew wide and lit up, and she felt like she could not contain the joy and happiness in her. She rushed into the living room and found Charlie sitting in a swing, cooing happily and looking around with her bright blue eyes and a wide baby grin.

"Oh my gosh! Look at her! She's gotten so big! How could she have grown so much? It hasn't been that long since I saw her! Oh... baby girl, my sweet, precious, beautiful baby girl. I've missed you so much!" She stopped the swing and lifted

Charlie out of it, nuzzling her nose and mouth into the baby's neck and soft dark curls of hair.

Charlie was delighted to see her, and cooed and kicked happily, waving her arms and staring with wide eyes. River Lea folded her arms around the baby and walked over to the sofa to sit down with her and hold her, talking to her and touching her face, her arms, and her hands. She kissed every bit of skin she could see, and loved every single moment of it just as much as the baby did.

Matthew watched them and made his way slowly to the couch, not taking his eyes off of them, even as he came to sit down next to them.

"She has gotten big," he said as he took in the sight of the two of them playing and talking to each other in their own way. Matthew shook his head as he stared at them. "I should have had you over here all the time, and I should have brought her to see you. I'd forgotten how close the two of you are."

He sounded regretful, but River Lea was anything but regretful at that moment. She was overwhelmed with pure bliss, and nothing could change it. She played with Charlie and held her until the little girl finally fell asleep on River Lea's chest.

River Lea rubbed her back soothingly, and looked over at Matthew. "Shall we put her down to bed?" she asked in a whisper.

He nodded and helped her up from the sofa. River Lea walked upstairs with him and it felt to her like she was home, rather than in a stranger's house, or even a friend's place. She felt like she was where she ought to be, and it felt good.

The two of them went into the nursery and laid the baby down in her crib, covering her with a light blanket. They watched her for long moments and then Matthew took River Lea's hand and led her quietly from the room.

They passed through his bedroom and she couldn't help but look at the bed and remember what they

251

had shared in that bed the last time she had been there. It made her heart beat faster just thinking about it.

Matthew took her downstairs to the kitchen and made a pot of coffee for them. She sat at the table and he began to talk with her as he was pulling mugs down from the cupboard and measuring out coffee grounds for the coffee pot.

"The lawyers have met with the judge, and there has been a change in our circumstances," he said with a tired voice. It was then that she realized just how worn out he looked, and how much of a toll the divorce was taking on him.

She hadn't seen it before because when she arrived at the house, he was so happy to see her, that it overshadowed everything else, but as the wave of excitement subsided and they relaxed, his weariness was much more evident to her, and it filled her with concern.

"What's changed?" she asked, not entirely sure that she really wanted to know.

He came and sat down beside her, waiting for the coffee to finish. "Well, her lawyer pleaded her case to the judge, and while my team was strong, her lawyer somehow created the pity party of the century, and the judge is going to allow shared custody during the divorce until he can make a decision about custody when the end of the divorce comes. For now, though, we have been ordered to share Charlie."

River Lea's mouth fell full open. "No…" she breathed out in not much more than a whisper.

He nodded. "Oh yes. There's no way to get around it." He got up and went to the coffee pot, pouring each of them a mug of the steaming beverage and then walking back to her. "What's more is that my team of attorneys sees this as a bad sign; if the judge is willing to give her shared custody now, it may be more difficult to get that revoked with the divorce becomes final and a permanent decision regarding custody is made. We'd be backtracking, whereas if he had said no to shared custody now, it

253

would be a good indicator of how things are going to go later on at the end."

She sighed and sipped her coffee, feeling sick at the idea of Amil having any kind of contact with Charlotte. "Can't your team tell the judge about how she hasn't ever been involved with her? Not at any point?"

He shrugged. "Well, they did, but that's a tricky point, see... neither of us was really involved until I spent that last month of the pregnancy with you, and even that wasn't supposed to happen. That only happened because of our special circumstances.

If we had gone according to the contract like we were supposed to, neither she nor I would have had anything to do with you at any point, or the baby until after the birth. So, in the eyes of the court, she wasn't even supposed to be around until Charlie was born, and that hasn't been that long. She's saying we were estranged and I was keeping the baby from her.

I have said that I wasn't, but she told the judge that I never even let her know when the baby was born. Unfortunately, that's true. I didn't tell her when Charlie was born, because I believed she wanted nothing to do with her."

"Oh no…" River Lea sighed and frowned at the realization of what he was explaining to her.

"The only real saving grace, and this is actually more of a problem with two sides of the same coin, is that you were here taking care of her and Amil never did, but that could easily be shown as a very negative thing. The good side of that is that no one knows you were here, except us. You were gone before the nanny was hired, and you haven't really been back since, so there's nothing at all to indicate that anything… untoward… has happened.

As far as the courts and the lawyers, and the ex knows, you gave birth to the baby and then went home, and that was that. So… we could leave it at that, or we could tell the courts that you came here and helped me to raise her for the first weeks of her life while her mother was out sleeping with another man. That could be taken well, and it could also backfire in a big way and destroy our entire argument." He sighed.

"I'm not sure what to do with it." He looked at her and a small smile flickered on his face.

All River Lea could think of were Gibby's words. "I think it's best if we wait to see what happens. Keep me as an ace if you need one, but see if you can get this whole thing swayed in your direction without me. As you said, using me could go either way. That's a big risk to take with your daughter."

He nodded. "Wisely said. I think I will take your advice and wait it out. I'll be honest, I'd like to think that my ex's track record is bad enough that the judge takes one look at the whole thing and tells her to leave with nothing, but that's a pie in the sky dream."

She laughed a little and shrugged. "Well, we'll see. We can hope."

He smiled again then, genuinely, and tipped his head as he looked at her thoughtfully. "It's so good to have you here. It's like... it feels like you've come home, and I hope that doesn't make you uncomfortable, but it just feels right to have you back here. I like it, a lot."

She grinned at him. "I was thinking the same thing as we were taking the baby up to put her down for her nap."

"You were?" he asked in surprise, and she nodded.

"Will I get to meet the nanny today?" River Lea asked him, trying to keep the conversation light and her eyes off of his face and chest. She hadn't missed the button-down shirt he was wearing which was partly opened, revealing places on his chest that she had kissed and tasted, or the strong arms which had held her so close to him. She was sure that all of the memories were coming back because they had walked through the bedroom together and she was doing her best to think of anything else.

He shook his head. "No, actually, she's not here today. It's her day off. She gets two days off a week and this is one of them. I'm sorry, I didn't think about that. I'd have liked to have you meet her."

River Lea took another long sip of her coffee. "What's she like?" she asked curiously.

Matthew shrugged. "She's nice. A little older. She's a British lady; she's kind and a little proper, but not stern or mean. Actually," he stood up and motioned for River Lea to follow him, "I'll show you a photograph of her."

They walked back into the living room, and he went to a table behind the sofa. There he picked up a framed photograph and handed it to her. In the photo was an older woman who looked like she could have been someone's favorite aunt. She was holding Charlie and they were both laughing and grinning, and River Lea got a good feeling about the woman just from looking at the captured moment in the image.

She smiled wide. "She looks like a nice lady. What's her name?"

Matthew looked at the image and smiled as well. "Her name is Hattie. She is a nice lady. We got a good one."

River Lea hesitated and then looked up at him with questioning eyes. "We?"

He looked into her sea blue eyes and took the frame from her hand, setting it back on the table without taking his eyes from her. "We," he said quietly. "You, and Charlie, and me. As far as I'm concerned, it's always going to be the three of us. So, yes. We."

River Lea bit her lip and her eyes grew wet with happy tears. Matthew saw it and looked worried for a moment.

"Don't cry!" he whispered, raising his hand to touch her cheek. "Please don't... cry..." he barely spoke as he wiped away one stray tear that made an escape through her thick black eyelashes.

He shook his head subtly, almost as if he was trying to remind himself of some kind of sense, but it didn't stop him. He leaned forward and touched his lips softly to hers, hesitantly at first, and she knew in that one instant that if she did not kiss him in return, he would end the kiss, and that would be that. They would go back to the platonic state that they found themselves in.

She kissed him back. She pressed her lips full against his, missing the feel of them, missing the feel of the electric heat between the two of them, and the moment that she kissed him back, a blazing bonfire ignited between the two of them.

His arms wrapped tightly around her and he crushed her to his body, his breath, like hers, growing shallow and short as they gasped and tasted one another, sucking and biting gently at one another's mouths as they kissed.

He groaned softly and she felt him grow hard against her. She knew there was nothing in her that had the strength to stop him, no matter what Gibby had said. His mouth trailed down her neck leaving flames its wake, and a soft moan escaped her.

The sound of it was all it took to push Matthew beyond his limit. He pulled at her dress until it was lying in a puddle of soft fabric on the floor, and he let his own clothes fall away from him. She kissed him hungrily, having ached for him and needed him more than she ever could have imagined she would.

He lowered her to the sofa, and though he tried to take his time with her, canvassing her body with his mouth, running his tongue and hands over her curves and lines, and even up inside of her enough that she came as his tongue twisted in her depths, he could not hold himself back from her for long, and as he pushed the length of himself into her body, she arched her back and cried out in pure pleasure as he began to move in her, filling her, making her tremble with ecstasy.

They held tightly to one another, their bodies giving and taking, responding as familiar lovers do, knowing where to touch and how, insatiably hungry for each other, needing to feel the fiery connection as the whole world falls away and they find that they are the only two beings in the universe. Matthew and River Lea held each other fast, and as he had before, he brought her to her fullness time and again, making her come over and over, until she could barely breathe or move, and it wasn't until then, when he had no more strength in him, that he let himself release his orgasm into her, growing weak as he was spent.

He kissed her softly, and held her close to his chest, his arms gentle and strong around her. "I didn't know if that was ever going to happen again," he whispered. "I wanted it to... God I have wanted it to, but I wasn't sure after you left the last time, if it would ever happen again."

She smiled at him and kissed his cheeks and his mouth softly. "I wanted it to happen again, too. I haven't been able to stop thinking about it, or to stop myself from wanting you, and needing you. It's so difficult to have so much desire for you and to lock it away and leave it untouched."

He agreed with a nod. "I know exactly what you mean. We never should have let this much time pass between us. This... whatever this is between us, it's something so powerful, I don't know how we can possibly deny it to ourselves."

He kissed her again, slowly and sweetly, and the kisses grew warmer and more passionate, until she felt him hard against her again and as he spread her thighs open once more and entered her, she knew exactly what it was.

"Matthew..." she whispered his name against his skin.

He looked down at her as they moved together and she kissed him tenderly. "It's love... for me... it's love." She kissed him once more. "I love you." She hadn't meant to say it, but it was how she was feeling, and it was the truest thing she had ever said.

He smiled as she looked up at him, and he kissed her in return. "I love you, too, my beautiful River Lea. I love you, too."

They made love for a long while, until they were lost in each other's arms again, and then they heard Charlie wake up, and they dressed quickly, giggling like teenagers trying not to be caught, and went up to take care of the baby girl.

All three of them went out beside the pool, sitting in the sun enjoying each other's company, and Matthew looked at River Lea seriously.

"What I said before about this being your home… I meant it. I want you to stay here, River. I want you to be here with us. Live here. Please… I know it might seem like we're moving fast, but it feels like that's the way it's supposed to be. I want you here, and I know this little girl does, too." he looked at her earnestly and she felt a twinge of regret in her heart.

She might not have been able to resist making love with him again, but she knew for certain that anything more than that would be a step in the wrong direction for them.

"Matthew, I'd love nothing better than that, but this isn't a good time for us to talk about that. Think of the divorce! What a mess that would cause. How would we explain that? You'd lose Charlotte so fast. It's not worth it. I think the best thing that we can do is wait to see what happens in court, and when it's all said and done, no matter how it goes, then maybe we can talk about things moving forward with you and me, but this is the worst possible time for that to happen for you." She hoped that he wouldn't feel rejected, and that he could see the logic and reasoning in her response.

He was quiet a long moment, frowning as he considered it, and at first she wasn't sure how he would take it, but then she saw him nod and his shoulders sagged a little in resignation. "I know you're right. I know it in my head… it's the best thing to do, and it's the safest thing to do, but I know I can't convince my heart of that. I want you here, with me, not down the road half an hour. I want you here in my bed, in my arms, in my home, in my life… all the time. I don't want you to leave." He sighed heavily.

Looking up at her, he took River Lea's hand in his. "I guess for now though, as long as you know that, that will have to be enough, and as long as you know that I'm not going to stop or settle until someday you are here with me… I guess I can be patient and hold off on trying to make it happen until the timing is right."

She smiled and nodded in return and raised his hand to her lips to kiss his fingers. "It will wait, and I think it will make the realization of it even sweeter when it does happen. Until then, I will know in my heart that that's what you truly want, and you will know in your heart that I want exactly the same thing, and we'll just keep the dream safe in our hearts until that time."

Matthew smiled at her then, and rubbed his finger over the back of her hand. "You're an amazing lady, and I'm so lucky to have found you, and even luckier still that you love me."

It was incredible to her that they were using the word love, and meaning it with the depth that they did, but she was glad that they had finally reached that point with one another, and she cherished it.

They spent the day together with the baby, loving the precious fleeting time that they shared, wishing that they could have more, but simultaneously being grateful for every moment they got to have.

When the afternoon grew late, River Lea told them goodbye and headed home. She kept thinking of what he had requested of her all the way home. She thought of how he had pleaded with her to live there with him, and how much he wanted it, and how much she also wished it could be that way, and by the time she got to her house, she wasn't entirely sure that they should wait. She wondered about how it might go in court, because it could go any way.

She called Gibby to talk with him about it, and he was glad to hear from her.

"I was over at Matthew's today," she admitted to him. "I got to spend time with the baby, and I… spent time alone with Matthew… and it was incredible. I missed him so much. I can't explain how amazing it feels to be with him. I can't seem to get enough of it; I just want him more and more. I even told him that I love him, and you know what? He said it back to me. He loves me too." She felt almost defiant, saying all of it to Gibby.

He sighed. "This isn't good, my dear. The timing probably couldn't be worse."

She frowned and bit at her lower lip. "I know that. We talked about it. He wants me to move in with him, and live there. He wants us to basically be a family. I thought about what you've told me and how that wouldn't be a great idea right now, and that's what I told him, you know, that we have to wait until after the divorce, but I'm not entirely sure that's the best idea! Maybe he's right. Maybe I should move in now."

Gibby hummed a no. "Uh uh, honey. What's going on with his divorce? Is it finished yet?"

River Lea felt sadness creeping in around her. She knew her best friend was going to reason her out of her daydream. "No," she told him honestly. "Actually, they're kind of losing the battle a little bit right now. The ex-wife wants shared custody of the baby, and the judge is giving it to her, just until the divorce is final. So, she gets the baby half of the time from now until a final decision is made about custody."

"And you think this is a good time to move in to his house? What do you think is going to happen in court if the judge has already shown favor to her requests and has given her shared custody of Charlotte? If you move in now, you might as well give that baby up for good.

The judge isn't going to look kindly on the father's girlfriend moving in, especially if that girlfriend just happens to be the surrogate mother of the baby they just had. That has suspicion and extra-marital affair written all over it, and you don't need that, and he sure as hell doesn't need that. Neither one of you are thinking clearly about anything.

What is going on in your mind? Don't help her case like that. You can't do that! Let that crazy woman hang herself. She will do it if you give her enough rope, but if you two don't hold off until this whole thing is done, you're going to shoot yourselves in the foot, and wreck it all!" He huffed at the end in exasperation and she knew she had gone too far.

Sighing, she agreed with him, knowing with everything in her that he was right. "Yeah, I know. I know. I didn't really think about it that way. I just… I want him so much, but you said it before; if we wait, we could really save ourselves all kinds of headache and heartache, and stop any kind of problems from developing in the courtroom. I guess it would look bad to have me around; even if I am there taking care of the baby."

"Doesn't he have a nanny? Didn't he hire a nanny?" Gibby asked, still on his warpath.

"Yes, he has a nanny," she answered him.

"Well, that's all he needs to do to show the court that he's taking good care of that baby. He's got himself and the nanny, and his ex has left the building, so the only thing that could screw this up from here forward is if you get into the picture. Stay out of the picture. Totally. Completely.

Focus on school and don't even talk to him until this thing is over, and then you can go over and have happy family love, but in the meantime, you're going to destroy his chances if you put even one toe in it. Stay out of it!" his tone was serious and he was firm, though not unloving about it.

River Lea felt a sadness saturate her heart. "I know you're right."

"That's because I am right," he replied shortly. "So listen to me."

"I will. I guess I knew that all along, but I kind of hoped I could do something to help him win the case." She hoped that she didn't sound as dejected as she felt.

"You can! You can stay the hell out of his life until the whole thing is over, and then you can get back into it again, and it will all be good and happy and wonderful, but not before!" he insisted.

"Okay. I'll stay out of his life until the divorce is done," she acquiesced reluctantly.

"Good girl. Just stay strong and listen to me, and don't cave to desire. Follow through on this," he added with kinder tone.

"I will. Thank you for listening to me and talking this through with me," she said, a smile turning up the corners of her mouth.

"You got it, my dear. I'm always here for you." He sounded happy again. She asked him how things were going with Brad and he launched into all of his latest with his boyfriend, and the conversation became considerably lighter.

When the call was finished, she thought again of just how lucky she was to have him, and how different her life would be without him there to support her. She wouldn't trade him for the whole wide world.

***

A week passed, and she hadn't heard much of anything from Matthew, but that was the way they had agreed to leave it. She had talked to him briefly after her phone call with Gibby, and she told him everything that Gibby had said. He agreed that it was most likely for the best that they keep things cool and distant between them as much as they could while the divorce was going on.

It surprised her then, when she saw that he was calling her late one evening; much later than she ever would have expected him to call. It was nearly eleven at night.

Panic flushed through her and she answered the phone right away. "Hello? Matthew?" She held her breath as she waited to hear what he had to say.

His voice sounded torn, as if he himself was in tattered pieces and she was only able to hear part of him because he wasn't wholly himself. "River Lea! River... God... I can't believe this.... I'm... I can't believe this." He tried to speak, but his thoughts and his words were as broken as his voice.

She sat bolt upright in bed and clutched the phone in her hand. "What's going on? Where are you?"

He tried to catch his breath and speak slowly to her, and she could hear him struggling. "I'm... I'm in the hospital!" he said thickly.

River Lea leapt from her bed and began to try to find clothes to wear, pulling them on as she listened to him on the phone. "You are? What happened to you? Are you all right?"

There was a sob at the other end of the line and then it was quiet and she heard him drawing in his breath slowly. "It's not me. It's Charlie."

River Lea's heart stopped in her chest and she froze in place, her jeans pulled halfway up her legs, the phone sealed tightly on her ear. "What? What... happened?" Her mind shot out suddenly in countless different directions. The baby must have fallen, or choked, or had an allergic reaction. She didn't know what it could be, and every thought from simple to horrifying crossed her mind all in a split second.

"What is it?" she asked breathlessly in her panicked stated.

He tried to calm himself enough to speak. "Amil took the baby today… it was her turn for a visit, and she left with her this afternoon. I guess she went to some friend's house and she was drinking…" He stopped and had to collect himself again, and the words he spoke began to burn through River Lea as she stood there frozen. They heated her up and she began to grow angry so deeply inside of herself that she moved even faster than she had before. She was dressed and rushing around to grab her keys and wallet as he continued to talk.

"She left her friend's house drunk and…" he paused again to breathe, "she got into a car wreck. She rolled her car. Charlotte was in her car seat, thank God, but she was hurt. She was cut by broken glass." He stopped and she could hear that he was trying to catch his breath again.

"Oh my God… is she all right?" Tears stung her eyes and her heart felt like it was going to break in half right in her chest.

"Charlotte will be all right. The cuts aren't too bad, but she hasn't stopped crying, my poor baby girl; she's terrified, and there's blood… there's so much blood…" he began to choke on tears and River Lea tried to talk to him and get him to focus on her voice as she climbed into her car.

"I'm on my way, Matthew. I'm in the car. Just tell me which hospital you're at." She tried to speak as calmly as she could, but inside all she could see was her little Charlotte, bloodied and broken.

"I'm at Memorial," he told her, and she set her car on the road in an immediate rush.

"What happened to Amil?" she asked, wondering if the woman made it through all right. She knew it would be hard on Matthew if anything had happened to her, even in the midst of their divorce.

His voice grew venomous. "Amil…. She's fine. Not a scratch on her. They arrested her and brought her here to the hospital so that as soon as she sobers up she can give blood to the baby."

River Lea was furious. *Of course Amil was fine*, she thought. It was the baby who was suffering because of her selfish stupidity. She tried to remain as calm as she could so that she could focus on driving safely, and as soon as she got the room location from Matthew, she hung up and gave all of her attention to the road in front of her.

In almost no time at all she was parked outside of the hospital and on her way into it. She found Matthew and he almost leaped from his chair when she walked into the waiting room at the nursery. He wrapped his arms around her tightly and held her, and it was only then that they both let themselves cry together, holding each other for support until they were able to steady themselves.

She looked up at him and asked where the baby was. He walked with her to the area where she was being kept. She was hooked up to machines that beeped and chattered, and River Lea was sure that she had never seen a sadder sight than the little girl she had carried and given birth to, lying there asleep with bandages on her body and tubes coming out of her in so many places.

She almost choked on her tears. "I thought you said she was fine!" She stared in horror at the baby and Matthew was going to speak, but the doctor came to them just then.

"She is fine, or at least, she will be. She went through quite a traumatic experience tonight, but she was asleep when it happened, so her muscles weren't tightened when the vehicle rolled. She woke up afterward, and the unfamiliarity of everything around her upset her quite a bit. We've only just gotten her calmed down and resting. That's going to help her more than just about anything. There are some abrasions around her body, but she'll recover, and I believe she's going to be lucky and that none of the cuts will scar. We'll see how it all heals." He looked at them both then, his kindly old eyes appeared to be troubled.

"May I ask who you are?" he queried, looking at River Lea. "Are you family, by chance?"

She hesitated and Matthew stepped in for her. "Yes, she is, actually. She is the surrogate mother who carried this baby for my ex-wife and me."

The doctor raised his eyebrows and pushed his lips out thoughtfully. 'Is she now? Well… that's interesting. It's very interesting indeed." He folded his hands in front of him and looked at River Lea keenly.

"Tell me, young lady, would you be willing to donate some blood for this little one? I have a feeling that we may be a bit surprised by what we find, and this little young lady here is in pretty desperate need of some blood." He looked over the top of his glasses at River Lea, and River Lea nodded back immediately to him.

"Of course! I'd be glad to!" She followed the doctor and he stayed with her as the nurse drew blood from her and then took it to run some quick tests. When she came back, she conferred with the doctor and the doctor nodded quietly and came to River Lea and Matthew with a serious expression on his face.

"The nurse is going to want a quart of blood from you, my dear," he began quietly.

"No problem. I'm glad to give it," River Lea answered promptly. The nurse sat her in a chair and tied a rubber strap around her upper arm right away.

Matthew and River Lea looked up at the doctor then, and he sighed heavily. "I have to tell you both something, and I'm sorry to have to be the one to break it to you. It seems that Amil Chase's blood does not match the baby's blood at all. We cannot use Amil's blood for her. Yours however, River Lea, is a perfect match for the baby's."

They looked at him in surprise, both of them staring, unblinking, trying to comprehend what he was saying. His old white cheeks turned a pale pink as he continued. "It is not possible that this baby is in any way Amil's natural daughter. This little girl's biological parents are the two of you." He said, looking from Matthew to River Lea as he became quiet.

They stared at him. "How can that be? That's not possible…" River Lea said in a shallow voice as the shock of his statement tried to work its way through her mind.

Matthew shook his head. "It isn't possible. Amil and I went to the clinic to have our baby created and River Lea is the surrogate. That's all; she just carried the baby. The baby is biologically hers and mine." Matthew seemed to try to be correcting the doctor.

The doctor shook his head at them. "I promise you, there is no way that this child has any biological connection to Amil; none whatsoever. She is the natural daughter of you two. Perhaps you may want to speak with the clinic when they open in the morning. In the meantime, Miss River Lea, thank you for the blood. Your daughter desperately needed it."

With that, he left them and they turned to one another and stared at each other with disbelieving eyes. They both tried to speak, to question, to ask… but neither one of them could manage to make any sense of it.

Later that morning, they stood together in the waiting room of the hospital, and called the fertility clinic together. When they finally got the doctor on the phone with them, they explained what had happened. The doctor at the other end of the line hemmed and hawed for a few minutes, trying to get out of answering questions, but when Matthew grew angry and threatened to bring his lawyers into the situation, the doctor confessed.

He told them that Amil had come to him after the initial meeting and explained to him that she did not want a biological child. She told him that it was all Matthew's idea and she truly wanted no part of it. She paid the doctor off with an enormous sum of money and told him to just use one of the surrogates eggs as both Amil and the surrogate were of African American heritage. Matthew understood then why she had insisted on the surrogate mother being of the same race as she was; a point of demand of hers that he had never fully understood.

The doctor had taken one of River Lea's eggs then, and combined it with Matthew's sperm, and the result had been Charlotte, who truthfully had no biological connection to Amil whatsoever. The doctor apologized profusely to them and told him how sorry he was about what he had done. He explained that he never would have done it normally, except that Amil was so adamant about not having the baby be hers naturally, and she had paid him an exorbitant sum of money.

Matthew insisted that the doctor write out a statement declaring exactly what he had told them, and if he received the statement signed in ink that day, he would not press any charges or seek legal retribution, which would unquestionably get the clinic shut down permanently. The doctor agreed to send the letter by courier to Matthew that same day, and when Matthew ended the phone call, he walked over to the window overlooking a grassy area, and slid his hands into his pockets.

River Lea felt horrible for him, and walked up behind him, placing her hands upon his shoulders. "Matthew, I'm so sorry." She spoke softly. "I can't imagine what you're going through right now. This is such a... such a shock."

He turned to her then, looking at her in surprise. "It is a shock, but it's just as much a shock for me as it is for you. You have a biological child that you weren't aware of at all. That's... amazing," he told her, almost in disbelief still.

"Do you know what this means?" he asked, lifting his hands to her shoulders and holding her close to him.

"What?" she asked, blinking up at him.

He grinned. "It means every possible good thing. It means that those beautiful blue eyes of hers are yours, and that makes me love her even more, which I didn't think was possible." River Lea gasped and a grin stole over her face as she realized that he was speaking the truth. Charlotte was her baby; her real baby, and her baby girl had the same sea blue eyes as she did.

"It means that when I get that letter from the doctor at the clinic today, I can give it to my attorney and the judge will hopefully revoke any and all parental rights from Amil, seeing as it's not her child." He grinned and couldn't hold back a laugh. River Lea laughed with him and sighed in wonder.

"It means a lot more than that… but we can talk about that later. For now, let's go spend some time with our daughter." He blinked back tears and River Lea found herself walking as if she was on clouds, holding on to Matthew's hand as they made their way back to the nursery.

It was two more days before the doctor let them take Charlotte home, but the baby had been in much better spirits being with her parents, and it seemed that the doctor was right and that none of the scrapes and cuts would scar her tender skin.

The letter from the doctor at the clinic arrived when it was supposed to, and Matthew took it to his team of lawyers personally. They requested a special meeting with the judge, and the judge granted a hearing scheduled for two days from the date of the request.

Matthew insisted that River Lea come home with him to help him take care of Charlotte, and she went willingly and happily with him. He took her to his bed that night and made love to her all through the night, holding her and kissing her more tenderly than he ever had, and when at last they were resting in each other's embrace, he looked at her and spoke quietly to her.

"I want you to move in here with me. There is no reason for you to wait any longer. Charlotte doesn't have any connection to Amil; we can't lose our baby girl to that evil woman, so there's nothing else to worry about. I need you here with me. I want you to move in as soon as you can. I want you to make this a permanent change and be here with Charlotte and me as a family." He paused and watched her carefully. "Please… say yes."

She was silent, trying to swallow her emotion and find some way to answer him if she could make her voice work for her.

"Say something… please?" he asked, looking at her questioningly.

She grinned and her voice came to her at last. "Yes… yes, I will come here and live with you. I will make this a family with you."

He cried out with joy and wrapped his arms around her, holding her tightly to him. They finally fell asleep with each other and discovered that their sweetest dreams were already real.

River Lea called Gibby the next morning and spent an hour with him on the phone explaining everything that had happened, and telling him that he really was Charlie's uncle. He was thrilled and relieved to hear the news, and he was finally happy to support her moving in with Matthew.

Two days passed and they all went to the court hearing together to see the judge. When Matthew had mentioned having a team of lawyers, she hadn't really thought about how many there were, but standing together at the table when they walked in were five men in tailored suits and every one of them was on the case. They welcomed River Lea and congratulated her on the news of her daughter.

River Lea looked across the room as Amil and her attorney walked in the door. Amil looked miserable and angry, but not nearly as angry as River Lea was. Matthew reached for her hand and held her back as Amil breezed past them like they weren't there at all and took her seat.

The judge entered the room and everyone rose as he took his seat, and then they all followed suit. He looked down at the file before him and then back up at the parties who were waiting to hear him speak.

"Does either council have anything to say that has not already been added to this file before me?" he asked, looking as if he was barely keeping his temper in check. Both sides said no. The judge looked down at all of it again and gave a disgusted snort. He pulled his glasses off and laid them carefully on the desk in front of him and then looked down at Amil.

"Amil Chase, I have seen a lot of things in my days and years on this bench, and in that time I have seen people pass before me who seem to be the lowest level of humanity in the human race. You fall very close to that level. I am disgusted to see that you have requested so much from this court, and none of it is yours. You asked for all of Mr. Chase's property; property which he bought from the proceeds of his company, a company which you have done nothing to build… a company which you deserted to go be with your husband's competitor.

You asked for all of his company. You asked for most of his financial assets. You asked for the child that he believed the two of you brought into this world. A child who is no more yours than mine. A child who exists because of your backhanded trickery and fraudulent ways. You want this child so that you can collect child support for it, but you never wanted the child to begin with."

He glared down at her hotly from his seat. "Mrs. Amil Chase, I am beyond disgusted with everything you have brought before this court. I have got to say, I've never seen a more selfish woman try to steal away what is not hers. It is this court's decision that every request made by Mrs. Chase be denied, except that of her name. Mrs. Chase, you will be given your maiden name, and that is all. It is all that you came into the marriage with, and it is all you shall leave with.

You do not deserve to have the last name of Chase connected whatsoever with your name. Therefore your every request save that of the return of your name is hereby denied. Mr. Chase," he said loudly, turning his attention to the other table, "I hereby grant you alimony to be paid monthly by your ex-wife until such time as you are married again or you become deceased. I'll set the amount in the decree. I wish you the best of luck, Sir, and congratulations on your divorce. Divorce granted." He slammed his gavel down and the bang echoed through the room.

Amil burst into tears and sobbed loudly as if the entire world had just come to an end, but Matthew and River Lea hugged each other tightly and thanked the judge before leaving the courtroom together.

The nanny was waiting for them outside with Charlie in her stroller, and they all decided to go to lunch together to celebrate.

***

Two months passed and Matthew was walking on their private beach with River Lea as they enjoyed the sunset. He was holding her hand, and she felt like she was walking on clouds again. He glanced over at her and raised an eyebrow.

"Is Gibby all moved in to your home yet? Totally settled?" he asked lightly.

She grinned. She had agreed to move Gibby and Brad into her house so they could live there and enjoy it, since she was living with Matthew.

"Yes, they are moved in and settled down. Hopefully happily ever after." She giggled and winked at Matthew.

He stopped walking then and turned to look at her fully. "Good. Then there is no chance you can escape back to your house."

Her smile faltered some and she looked at him in surprise, wondering why he might think she would want to escape. Before she could ask him, he lowered himself down to one knee and held out a ring to her. It was an enormous diamond set in platinum, and it sparkled dazzlingly in the late golden sunlight.

"I want you with me forever, River Lea," he said with a wide smile. "Take this ring, and promise me that you will be my wife. Promise me that you will spend every day of the rest of your life with me, and let me love you until we are gone from this world."

Her heart caught in her chest and she could barely breathe as she looked at him and tears flooded her eyes. She reached her hand slowly toward his and took the ring from him, looking at it in wonder. He wanted to marry her. He wanted to love her and keep her with him forever.

"There's nothing I want more than to be with you for the rest of my life," she answered him with her heart alight in flames of happiness and love.

He rose up from the ground and pulled her into his embrace, kissing her passionately as the last of the sunset colored the sky.

"I love you, River Lea," he breathed in-between kisses.

She grinned again and looked up at him. "I love you

too, Matthew," she answered softly, and then kissed him again.

Epilogue

Matthew and River Lea strolled down the beach, stopping every few feet as Charlie ran back and forth around them through the sand, picking up seashells and bringing each special one to them to hold for her until they could be taken to the house, cleaned, and set into her sea shell garden.

Both of her parents had their pockets and their hands full, and she continued to run and frolic in the shallow surf that brought her endless amounts of seashells and joy, and she continued to bring as many of the best sea shells to her parents as she could find.

River Lea filled the last of the space in her pockets and sighed, leaning backward with her hands on her hips. Matthew looked at her carefully.

"How are you two doing?" he asked with a steady gaze on her. His eyes dropped from hers to the mass of pregnant belly she was rubbing her hands over.

"Oh, we're fine. Grayson is just moving around and trying to make some room in there. He's so big now that he doesn't have much space to do anything, poor boy." She smiled and Matthew leaned over to kiss her gently.

"He'll be here soon, and then his big sister can teach him all about the fine art of sea shell collecting." He laughed, and River Lea laughed with him as Charlie ran up to them again, her small hands filled with sea shells and treasures that had to be kept.

"Maybe she'll grow up to be a marine biologist just like her mom," River Lea replied with a wink. Just then two men came down the pathway to the beach and Charlie squealed with delight, running to them.

"Unca Brad! Unca Gibby!" She lost herself in their arms and then dragged them both down to the shoreline where the waves were washing in new shells. She enlisted their immediate help in finding all the best ones, teaching them about which ones were most important.

"Look at this big, happy family," River Lea said with a laugh. "I'm the luckiest girl in the world."

Matthew wrapped his arms around her and kissed her cheek, and she knew as deep as her soul that it was true.

THE END

Message From The Author:

Hiii

I hope you enjoyed the main book.

As promised and as part of this special package there is a bonus book included that has never previously been released anywhere before and you can start reading this now on the next page!

THE BILLIONAIRE'S CONVENIENT SURROGATE

LENA SKYE

About This Book:

Billionaire casino owner Parker Spesato was having a hard time finding a suitable surrogate to give him the child he has always wanted. Whilst at the same time Alexandria Frey was looking for a way out of her abusive relationship and was willing to do anything to make enough money to escape.

When Parker proposed that Alexandria be his surrogate mother it seemed to be an arrangement based more on convenience than perfection but it seems that both of them have nothing to lose but possibly everything to gain...

THE BILLIONAIRE'S CONVENIENT SURROGATE

Chapter One

Alexandria

My hands were shaking as I grabbed as many clothes as I could from my drawers and closet and stuffed them into my suitcases. I didn't have much time before Roland got back from work and I couldn't be there when he did. I wouldn't let what happened last night happen again, I just wouldn't. I had managed to pack all of my clothes and went to close the dresser drawers.

I caught a glimpse of my face in the mirror and winced. The bruises were worse than last night. There were purple ones just behind my left eye, under the right side of my jaw, and dark ones around my neck. My adrenaline was pumping so, thankfully, I still couldn't feel them at the moment. Though the sharp pain in my side was hard to ignore, I forced myself to work through it. I hurried into the bathroom and grabbed my toiletries and then stuffed them into the remaining open suitcase and zipped it shut.

I pulled both suitcases off the bed and then hurried out to my car to load them into the trunk. I checked my watch and my heart nearly seized up, Roland was probably right around the corner. I hurried into the driver's seat and started the engine. I didn't have time to let the car heat up and prayed that the early Nevada winter cold wouldn't hold me back. Thankfully, my car went into gear and ran smoothly as I sped down the drive and then floored it down the street. I kept checking my rear view for signs of Roland or his truck and thankfully saw nothing.

I didn't know where I was going, but I knew that I had to get away from Roland. I needed to get all of my money out of Roland's and my joint account; he wasn't above freezing my money to get me to go back to him. I went to my usual bank on the corner, so that Roland had less of a chance to pick up my trail elsewhere. Then emptied my bank account and hurried on my way. I didn't exactly want to leave town just yet, I was nearly done with nursing school and I'd have a better chance at starting fresh somewhere else if I at least had my nursing license and degree.

I decided to check into a hotel. Boy, the apologetic faces of everyone I encountered at the front desk and on the way up to my room made it all real for me. I was running away from my abusive boyfriend. But Roland wasn't the type; he's never been…until last night. I didn't even know what I did to make him snap like he did. Just thinking about how angry he got made me wince. Then I felt the pain of all my bruises and I groaned. I needed to stick my face in a bucket of ice or something. I grabbed the ice bucket that sat on the desk in the hotel room and was just about to go fill it when my cell phone rang. I walked over to it and saw that it was Roland calling me. I hesitated before deciding to answer it.

"Where are you?" he barked into the phone

and I flinched at the anger in his booming voice.

"It's over, Roland," I said with surprisingly little waver to my voice. Anger surged to the surface and strengthened my voice even more. "I should have called the cops on you last night, but I will if you keep calling me. This is the last time, it's over," I said with finality and didn't wait for his hot blooded retort.

I hung up on him and threw my phone onto the bed with enough force to send it bouncing into the air and clashing with the wall to the right. I took a deep breath and then winced at the pain in my side. With another, softer breath I grabbed the ice bucket and then went to fill it up down the hall. When I got back to the room, I filled some small face towels to ice my bruises. I needed to try and calm down and regroup, though as soon as I laid down in bed, my eyes closed and sleep came over me almost instantly.

Come morning, I remembered I had work and I needed to make sure I changed where my paychecks got deposited. It was almost impossible to cover up my bruises with makeup. I gave up and decided to brush forward my dark brown hair instead and hoped that covered up the majority of bruising. I drove to work with the mindset of going in to talk with my boss about my paycheck. I was an orderly at a hospital in southern Paradise, which was near Las Vegas. The hospital was always busy, so I mostly hoped to simply *find* my boss. As soon as I pulled into my parking space in the garage, I heard a loud bang against the trunk of my car and I yelped in terror. My heart leapt into my throat and I turned to look over my shoulder.

There was Roland standing at the back of my car. He was wearing a black jacket and dark jeans; his blond hair was unruly when he usually kept it perfectly combed. His big build looked all the more menacing for the expression on his usually easy going and handsome face.

"Get out of the car Alex, let's talk," he called to me and I glanced around the garage and prayed for at least another car to drive through. But we were alone with rows of dead cars. "I just want to talk

305

Alex, you owe me that. You can't just up and leave me," he said, his voice grew hoarse and I looked at his expression through the rear view mirror. His green eyes looked emotionless, though he was trying to act as if he cared. Someone who could suddenly fly off the handle and beat me up wasn't someone who cared.

"Get away from my car, you fucking psychopath!" I yelled at him and made sure not to accidentally unlock my car doors. I put the car in reverse. I needed to call the cops on him or he would only continue to harass me.

"You don't have *anyone* here but me, I know you have no place to stay Alex, let's just talk about things," he barked and I lifted my foot off of the brake and began to ease back. "You're gonna run me over?" he yelled and I kept backing up until I got close enough to force him to back away.

"I should run you over for what you did to me! Leave me alone!" I yelled through the car window and once he was clear of the car, I sped away. I was perplexed to see him actually chase after me for a while until I was clear of the parking garage. I called in to work and made sure to talk to HR at least about my paycheck. Afterwards, I drove to the police station to go and file a restraining order. Thankfully, the lobby wasn't packed and I was able to go right up to the front desk.

"Yes, ma'am, how can I be of service?" The front desk officer was a warm woman and I almost cried on the spot at how sympathetically she looked at me.

"I'd like to file for a restraining order, please," I said. I couldn't help that my voice wavered, which only made the officer's expression soften even more.

"Have you been to the hospital, ma'am?" she asked me in concern. She had light brown hair that was pulled back into a ponytail, her eyes were sky blue and she had to have been the prettiest cop I'd ever seen.

"Um, no, I haven't…the bruises aren't as bad

as they look. I just…uh, I bruise easily," I said, stumbling over my words only a little.

"Well, I have to advise you to see a doctor just to double check, but we can start the filing process for that restraining order," she said and I breathed a small sigh of relief. I looked down at her badge; her name was Officer Trammel. She told me go on behind the door that separated the lobby from the actual offices. It was just like in the movies with the cubicles and officers sitting at their desks and working on cases. Trammel took some of my information down before she led me through the maze of officers.

Trammel led me to an officer's desk. He was a big stocky guy that reminded me of Roland a little bit. He had blond hair too, but dark brown eyes and less delicate features, more square and masculine.

"Officer Oden, this is Alexandria Frey, she wants to file for a restraining order."

Oden smiled at me with surprising warmth, just like Trammel. He reached out his hand and I shook it before he gestured for me to sit down at his desk.

"Thanks T, I've got it from here," he said and then she left me alone with Oden.

"So Miss Frey, do you want to start off by telling me what happened?" he asked and I took a deep breath.

"Well…the night before last I came home from work a little late. I work at Beth Memorial as an emergency room orderly and we were slammed just before my shift ended. I had to catch the next orderly up to speed before I left so…I got home about an hour late. Roland was at home—"

"I'm sorry, can I have his full name please?" Oden asked and I gave him Roland's full name and he wrote it down on a white pad. "Alright, please continue," Oden prompted me and I went on.

"So Roland was at home just…waiting for me. Usually, Tuesday nights are nights that I cook, but I had been late and Roland ended up cooking anyway.

He's usually an easy going guy, but that night…he was *angry*. He yelled at me—*screamed* at me for being late and then he threw a plate of food he had set out for me on the ground. He accused me of always working, of cheating on him…I was in shock. I thought he just had a bad day, so I told him to stop taking his crap out on me and that's when he really lost it. I didn't see his fists coming, one minute, I was standing by the breakfast bar, the next I was on the floor," I said and Oden nodded as he wrote down several quick notes.

"Alright, this is enough to get a restraining order filed, but is there anything else? Have you seen or heard from him again since the incident?" Oden asked and I told him about the phone call and then seeing Roland at work. "Okay, Miss Frey, all we have to do now is take a few pictures of your injuries and then we can get the paperwork filled out. Once that's done, if you'd also like to press battery charges, we can have a B.O.L.O put out for his arrest," Oden told me and I nodded, anything that would keep Roland away from me.

"Yes, anything, everything. I don't want him…near me ever again," I said and Oden nodded, his expression respectful, but his eyes seemed to approve of my decision.

"Don't worry Miss Frey, we'll throw the book at him," he assured me and I breathed an even deeper sigh of relief and went with him to go get the pictures taken.

I was at the police station for a few hours and when I got out, I could have sworn I spotted Roland's dark grey Silverado parked across the street on the curb. When I glanced over again, I saw the truck pull away and had no real way of telling since I was pretty far away. I hoped to God that I was only paranoid and that Roland hadn't completely flown off the handle.

Just to be sure, when I got to my car, I made sure to circle the police station a few times before going to my hotel. I parked in the parking lot and hurried to get from my car to the hotel. Of course, I dropped my keys on the ground as I got out of the car. I quickly bent to pick them up and in my haste, I ended up kicking them underneath my car. I sighed deeply and reached around my tire to feel for them. Eventually, I grabbed a hold of them and straightened…. right into a rock solid chest.

"You think you can tell the cops about me and that will handle me?" Roland's voice was a low hiss in my ear.

My heart slammed in my chest and my blood turned to ice in my veins. I frantically looked around, but we were hidden in between cars and there weren't any people outside. If I screamed loud enough, though, I was sure someone from inside the hotel would hear me.

"Get away from me Roland, I filed a restraining order and I pressed charges, you'll be arrested soon," I told him in a shaky voice.

"You can think that all you want Alex. You can think I'm behind bars for that matter, but I'll be one step behind you. You think you can just up and leave me, Alex? I don't think so, not without a fight," he growled and I looked up into his eyes. His pupils were dilated and his expression was almost void of emotion, that's what sent a violent shiver up my spine. I didn't know Roland, not really, until Tuesday night, and even then I still don't know what he was fully capable of.

"L—leave me alone Roland," I said, my voice still shaky as my heart was hammering in my chest.

"Me? Never, you're mine and you'll remember it soon enough," he spat and I lunged to the right to try and bolt away from him. He caught my arm and nearly wrenched it from its socket. I screamed bloody murder then and he let me go as if I branded him. I ran inside to the hotel and bent over with my hands on my knees once I was past the sliding doors. I forced air into my lungs and focused on breathing until the rushing in my ears calmed and my heart slowed.

"Ma'am? Are you alright? Is everything alright?" I looked up and saw one of the front desk guys right next to me.

"Can I show you a picture of someone, and if you see him you'll call the cops right away?" I asked him as I straightened and he nodded quickly, his brown eyes wide.

"Of course, we can print out a picture of him and I'll let all the staff know at our next meeting," he said and I couldn't be more grateful.

"Thank you so much," I told him and he led me to an office behind the front desk.

After that was taken care of, I went up to my room and laid in bed, shaking. What if Roland was truly capable of dodging the cops? What would I do? I *needed* to get away from him. There was no other option, I couldn't take his threat lightly, not after what he did, not after what he was *doing*. I had to put nursing school on hold, I would have to quit my job and move…. Tears started to slip from the corners of my eyes. How did I not see that Roland was capable of all this? Now I was faced with uprooting my life and…I wasn't even sure if I had enough money to up and move and then enroll in another nursing school to finish out my last semester. Roland paid for rent at our house, he paid for food, he covered everything so that I could go to school and cover the cost.

If I went to work, he would be there…hell, now he even knew where I was staying! I hurried out of bed and then went to the window that overlooked the parking lot. After scanning it several times, I found no sign of Roland. I hurried down to my car and drove to a nearby park to try and clear my mind a bit. I walked for a while and eventually sat down on the side of the path that snaked through the park. The place was nice; it was more like a nature walk with a lot of trees and a large pond at the beginning of the trail.

"Alex Frey?"

I started at the female voice that called my attention from staring off into space. I hadn't realized that I sat down next to someone. She had bright red hair and clear blue eyes that fit perfectly with her fair skin and soft feminine features. I did recognize her.

"We go to the same college, you're in the nursing program right?" she asked me and my eyes widened with full recognition.

"Nicole, Nicole Greene right?" I asked and she nodded with a wide smile.

"Yeah, we had a procedures class together once, remember?" she asked and I nodded.

"I do, it's good to see you again," I said and then her eyes skittered from bruise to bruise on my face and neck.

"My god, Alex…what happened?" she asked me in true concern.

"Ah…um, it's a long—well, actually, it's not really a long story…" I said and trailed off. I wondered if I should just make an excuse and go, but part of me really needed to talk to someone.

"Alex, you can talk to me, I know we don't know each other all that well, but that makes it easier," she said and I took as deep a breath as I could muster. I felt really, really crappy.

"My boyfriend...he...he just went crazy and um...ever since, it seems like I can hardly get away from him," I said, I was on the verge of tears. I just wanted Roland to be locked away and the key melted down to nothing.

"Did you call the cops?" she asked me, her blue eyes looked moist and I wondered if she felt for me that deeply. We really did hardly know each other.

"I went to file a restraining order and to press charges, they put a warrant out for his arrest, but right after I left the police station he found me and he—he threatened me. He knows where I work and he knows where I'm staying now...I just don't know what to do. I need to get away, but it's not like I can just go back to work. What if he kidnaps me in the parking garage?" I stopped myself from babbling and forced myself to take another breath.

"I think I know a solution, though you have to

keep an open mind," Nicole said and she looked at me in earnest.

"O—kay…" I said slowly.

"Well first off, you can stay with me. Your boyfriend doesn't know me so you'd be safest at my place until he's picked up by the cops. I live alone and I have an extra room so frankly, unless you can convince me that you have a safe place to stay, I won't take no for an answer. Then I know of a good job that can make you enough money to start over."

I blinked at Nicole in shock and awe. She had to have a bit of angel blood in her veins because not just anyone would offer what she was to a veritable stranger. Sure, we sat together in class and hung out on campus a few times to study, but that was as far as it ever went.

"I don't—I don't—I don't know what to say," I stuttered and she shook her head.

"You don't have to say anything," she said and smiled at me, her gaze held no ill will in it whatsoever. She had to have been the most genuine person I had ever met. "So, let's make a plan, yeah?" she said and I almost laughed a little.

"Um, yeah, yeah let's make a plan." Honestly, I had no other choice. I was desperate and Nicole was offering me a way out that seemed to be a blessing sent from heaven right when I needed it.

Chapter 2

Parker

"Mister Spesato, your video conference starts in five minutes." Kelly's voice came through the intercom on the desk phone; I thanked my assistant quickly before going back to the quarterly report I was reading.

I had been engrossed in the numbers and almost forgot about the video board meeting I had. My casino was doing well and I was seriously considering expanding to Atlantic City and even Miami. From the report I was reading, I thought about mentioning it as something for the board to think about, just to plant the initial seeds before I really made my case. I swiveled in my desk chair to face the desk and turned on my computer monitor to set up for the conference. I was connected in two minutes, the meeting went on as usual…well, as usually as could be expected. I waited until near the end of the meeting to bring up what I had in mind.

"Before you all go, I have something that you'd perhaps like to think about," I said and all eyes were on me through the screen. I was forced to hold eye contact with the group and hated the looks of pity or sorrow or wariness I was in their gazes, as if I might break down into tears right there in front of them.

"Well, go ahead Spesato, I have an appointment to keep," Franklin, one of the eldest board members spoke up. Why my father insisted I keep him on the board, I never figured out, but Franklin was about ready to pass his seat to his son, which I was grateful for.

"With these numbers holding and increasing several quarters in a row now, I think it's time to consider opening one or two more locations...Atlantic City is looking for new casinos..." I said and the faces of the seven men and three women all seemed thoughtful, even Franklin. "Anyway it's just something to think about for now," I said and afterwards ended the meeting. After I ended the feed I called Kelly through intercom.

"Kell, that was my last obligation for the day, correct?"

"Yes sir, you're free to go," she said with a laugh to her voice.

I breathed a sigh of relief and stood up to pack some paperwork into my briefcase and was on my way. My phone rang as I reached the elevators leading down to the rest of the casino.

"Mom, how are you?" I answered when I saw it was her calling.

"Oh, me? I'm fine darling, I called to see how you're doing…what with it only being days after your father's funeral and I've yet to hear from you since then," she said and I stifled a sigh.

"I've been busy with the casino, Mom…you know how it is," I said and then rubbed my chest at the odd painful pressure that seemed to emerge whenever my father was even mentioned.

"You've been running that casino for years now, I'm sure you can figure out a way to manage a small vacation. I'm sure the board would understand, and your employees as well."

"Yes, Mom, but I don't *need* a vacation. Honestly, I'm fine. Dad was sick for a long time, I've prepared myself for his death for a while now," I said and stifled another sigh when I heard my mother's sniffling on the other line.

"Well, the least you could do is pay your grieving mother a visit right after the death of her husband. I need to see my son, a visit would cheer me up," she said, fully guilting me without shame.

"Okay, alright, I'll come see you, Mom," I sighed and her sniffling quieted.

"Perhaps bring Edward with you? You know how I adore him," she said and I rolled my eyes.

"Okay, I'll give him a call and we'll bring dinner," I said and she made a sound of protest.

"Oh, nonsense, there's so much food here I can hardly give it away quick enough," she said and I made a face of distaste.

"I don't want to eat condolence food mom, Ed and I will bring something," I said and she sighed.

"Alright fine, I'll be expecting you," she said and then hung up soon after. The elevator stopped on the ground floor of the casino and I walked quickly through the happy vacationers and gamblers to get to my car outside. The valet had the Jaguar ready for me and I tipped the kid who handed me my keys. Once I was in the car, I called Ed and pulled away from the casino to head home.

"Yo, Parker, what's up?" Ed answered on the first ring, his voice as easy going as ever.

Ed was more of a brother to me than a best friend and my mother often claimed him as her second son, more for his personality than his uncanny resemblance to the family. Ed and I shared the same wavy black hair and had similar green eyes. But we differed in stature. I was taller and a bit bulkier in muscle than Ed who was leaner, though somehow he managed to kick my ass whenever we worked out at the boxing gym twice a week.

"Mom wants us over for dinner tonight, do you have plans?" I asked and Ed laughed.

"No, in fact she just texted me—more like threatened me to come over with you tonight," he said and I simply shook my head.

Even in grief, my mother was still up to her usual antics.

"I can swing by your place in about an hour and we can carpool," he said and after we made our plans, I ended the call and drove quickly home. If I was visiting mom, I needed to get all my leftover work done because there wouldn't be time to do it later.

I pulled into the drive at home and closed the gate to the grounds behind me as I walked towards the front door. I paused a moment as I walked up the drive to take in the scenery behind the house. Some people thought living in the desert was crazy and much preferred the mountains or the beach, but I saw the beauty in the landscape and faraway mountains. I ended my moment of nature appreciation and hurried inside and went straight to my office. If I wanted to open another casino, I would need people I trusted to help run it and then when I grew old, who would I trust enough to run the entire enterprise? Getting another casino approved and built was the easy part compared to that dilemma. Maybe my father was right? Perhaps it was time I settled down and had a few sons to take over for *me* one day.

I hadn't realized the time flying by as I researched some things to begin planning for another casino. So when Edward popped his head into my office I almost startled out of the desk chair.

"Ha, did I scare you?" Edward laughed as he stepped inside fully.

"How the hell did you get into the house?" I asked and he laughed at my slightly bewildered expression.

"Man, you must be *really* preoccupied, you left the door open and I have a key for the gate remember?" Ed said and pushed his hair out of his face, he had one of those asymmetrical undercut haircuts that females fell all over the place for. He must have just come from work, too, because he was still dressed in a blue pinstriped suit.

"I am…I'm thinking about opening another casino," I said and his eyes widened slightly.

"Seriously? Like where?"

"Atlantic City, then who knows, maybe Miami," I said and Ed whistled.

"Sights set high, but it's totally doable. I'd go forward with it," he said and sat at the edge of my desk as I closed a few things out on the computer. Ed was co-owner of his own father's casino in the city. Technically, we were rivals, but Ed and I went to the same schools since pre-K; there was no getting around our being best friends.

"Yeah, but I just had the whole 'legacy' debate with myself," I said and Ed's head fell back slightly as he laughed.

"It shouldn't be a debate Parker, you need to settle down by now, what are you? Forty, already? It's definitely time to have some kids," Ed said and I punched his arm lightly.

"I'm thirty-four jackass," I said and Ed chuckled.

"I'm just sayin'…at least think about getting married if you're squeamish at the thought of kids. Lord knows I partly got married just to shut my dad up about settling down and making a family," Ed said and I snorted.

"Believe it or not, I'm more squeamish about the marriage part," I said and Ed sighed as he straightened to his feet.

"Well, maybe you should try that online dating stuff, apparently those websites make pretty good matches. There has to be at least *one* woman out there built to deal with your mood swings," Ed said and I rolled my eyes as I walked past him to head out.

"Whatever, I'll think about it. What are we picking up for dinner?" I asked as we stepped outside and I made sure to lock up behind me.

"I'm thinking sushi, I bet your mom would prefer it to all the casseroles and crap being dropped off at her place," Ed said and I nodded in agreement as we got into his Audi. We stopped by Mom's favorite sushi place before heading to her and dad's place. When Ed pulled up to the house, I took a deep breath before getting out of the car.

"You alright?" Ed asked me when he got out of the car, his gaze was steady and not joking at all. He knew I struggled with my dad's death even if I saw it coming for a year in advance and tried to convince everyone that I was fine.

"Yeah...I'm fine," I said and he gave me a look that said how much he knew that was bullshit.

"Come on, let's take your mom some sushi,"

he said and I followed him up to the front door of the old fashioned mansion. My house couldn't be more different from my childhood home. Mine was more contemporary and modern, whereas my parents' house was more ornate and what some people would call 'old money.'

"Knock, knock, Mom we're home!" Ed called as we walked into the house, the door held open by the maid. I smiled at Lisa and she inclined her head with a polite smile. Mom had hired a few new people to add on to the staff in the house after Dad died and I hadn't yet learned all their names.

"Have my sons finally come to visit their mother?"

I couldn't help but laugh at the nearly excited sound of my mom's voice as she came hurrying into the foyer.

"Mom, for the hundredth time, you didn't give birth to Ed," I sighed and she waved her hand dismissively as she greeted Ed first with a big hug.

Anna Spesato, my mother, looked oddly youthful in her late fifties. She was beautiful with her soft features, dark hair, and bright blue eyes. She was average height and had always been thin, she was honestly the perfect elite wife, but my mom had a vibrant personality and was one of the most genuine people I knew.

"That is still up for debate. I was heavily sedated when they pulled you out, the same could be true for Edward," she said and I simply smiled at her fondly as she came to give me a long tight hug.

"Yeah, and where's my mom to say any different?" Ed scoffed and my mom let me go to pat his cheek fondly.

"Precisely, now what did you two bring for dinner?" she asked and poked in the bags I held. "Oh, sushi! You read my mind," she said in delight and Edward beamed at her proudly.

"It was my idea, I figured you'd want something light," he said and I rolled my eyes. If Ed and I *were* actually related, he would definitely be the favorite child.

"Come, let's eat then," she said and we followed her back to the kitchen where we set everything out on the family dining table. "So how are you both, update me," she said and I felt her eyes on me as I focused on putting food onto my plate.

"Well, things are going great at Palace, as usual. Dad is on track for retirement in a few years and I can't wait to fully take over," Ed said and I looked up at mom who was watching me closely.

"That's wonderful, Ed, but you should always practice patience," she said to him and he nodded.

"Yeah, I know, but it's getting harder the closer we get to his retiring," Ed said and my mom gave him a few more words of wisdom.

"And you Parker? How have you been?" she asked me and I forced myself to smile at her. I didn't want her worrying about me on top of mourning for dad.

"I've been good, I'm looking into opening another casino in Atlantic city," I said and my mom nodded, her eyes widened with a small smile that played on her lips.

"That's wonderful! Your father hoped you would go in that direction," she said and that pressure emerged in my chest yet again; all I could do was focus on holding my smile and nod.

"Dude, c'mon, it's painful watching you. It's okay to cry for your dad...he...he *died*," Edward said, not unkindly and I sighed deeply and rubbed my chest.

"I don't need to cry...I mean, yeah, okay I'm sad that he's gone. But I'll be fine, I'll get through it. Just like you, Mom, okay? Don't worry about me," I spoke to her more than Ed and she nodded slowly, her eyes filling with tears. I almost cursed, I hated seeing my mom cry. She dabbed at her eyes with a napkin and there was a moment of silence at the table where we all sort of just stared at out plates.

"So uh…Parker is thinking about settling down too, Mom," Ed said and I rolled my eyes at him in exasperation, ever the big mouth. I took a sushi roll and ate it so that I wouldn't have to answer my mother's surprised expression.

"*Really*? Something must have changed in the cosmos, my son wants to settle down, finally!" she said and Ed laughed while I gave a mock long suffering sigh.

"I'm just…you know thinking about it," I mumbled and mom gave me a pointed look.

"You *know* it's what your father wanted. He wants to keep the casino, or casinos, in the family. That would require you to settle down you know," she said and I nodded.

"Yeah I know mom, which is why I'm thinking about it," I said and she continued to stare at me.

"So what are you thinking about exactly? Marriage? Adoption? Mail order wife? Surrogacy?"

she asked and both Ed and I choked on our food, though he ended up laughing, whereas I simply stared at my mom in shock.

"*Mail order wife?*" I asked and she shrugged nonchalantly.

"I read, you know; these things exist," she said and I took a drink of fruit punch and shook my head back and forth.

"No, Mom, I'm not thinking about getting a 'mail order wife,'" I said and Ed started snickering all over again.

"Well, I know you don't exactly keep relationships with women for very long. Getting married may take a while for you and having a grandchild would be amazing, Parker," she said and then took a bite of her food, finally. I wondered if she was eating much and made a note to visit her with dinner more often.

"So what are you suggesting? That I use a...surrogacy program?" I asked and she didn't say anything, but gave me a look that said it all.

"You know, that's not a bad idea at all, it's reputable and you could have a kid right away without having to deal with getting married first. I think it's a good plan for you Parker," Ed said and I looked at him in slight disbelief.

"You think it's a good idea, really?" I asked him and he shrugged, I glanced at my mom again, who seemed to be preoccupied with her food at the moment.

"So I should…I could have a kid…right now…" I entertained the idea and found it surprising at how easily I could picture having a nursery in the house and a little toddler running around. Having a baby would not only solve the family business problem, but it would bring a lot of happiness into our lives. Mine and my mom's, probably even Ed's.

"I could see you being a dad, Parker, a husband…not so much. Kind of like my dad," Ed said and my mom nodded.

"Yes, I see it as well. Remember Yappy?" My mom reminded me of my childhood pet. Yappy was a Yorkshire terrier and lived to be a good old twenty years old. I grew up with him and often treated him like my kid.

"Think about it, it's something to seriously consider," Mom said and I nodded.

"Alright, I'll research it and...stuff," I said and thankfully that was the end of that conversation.

Chapter Three

Alexandria

"So that's all you have to do to sign up to register. Soon, someone will call you to get you fully checked out and registered as a surrogate," Nicole said and I sat back on the couch with a sigh.

"That was…disturbingly easy," I said and she laughed.

"Well, the hard part comes when you have to go to the doctor and get all these sorts of checks and physicals. Then, afterward, if someone actually picks you to carry their baby. Like I said the money doesn't start coming until there's a heartbeat," Nicole said and I nodded.

She explained it enough that I was sure I could convince a complete stranger to become a surrogate mother. Though I still had to convince myself that what I was resorting to wasn't really crazy. I was helping some future couple have a baby and the money was exactly what I needed to start over far, far away from Roland. I stared at the computer on the coffee table for a while, debating my decision, but really, what other choice did I have?

"Hey, Alex…you okay there?" Nicole waved her hand in front of my face and I shook myself out of my internal debate. It was done anyway, there was no real going back.

"Yeah, yeah…I'm just…I was just thinking," I said and she gave me a patient look.

"Don't worry Alex, if you're all checked out and someone picks you to be their surrogate, just think, in a year you could be home free," she said and I nodded.

"Yeah, you're right. I just have to focus on the future," I said with resolve and Nicole smiled at me almost proudly.

"Great, so do you want to maybe go get a bit to eat? I know of this great place, it's a drive so I

339

figure we won't have any chance of running into Roland," she said hopefully and I smiled at her. What I did to deserve her kindness was beyond me.

"Sure, that sounds great." Honestly, I was more looking forward to getting out of the house than going to eat. Nicole took charge of my situation almost as if she's had some sort of training in dealing with domestic abuse situations.

"I know you need to get out after being cooped up for a few days, but you do know it was necessary," Nicole said and I stood up and followed her to the front door. I grabbed my purse from the small table next to the front door and she grabbed hers, as well as her car keys.

"Yeah, I know, honestly you thought of everything, I don't think Roland will find me here," I said and she nodded with a determined smile.

"He won't, it would be impossible. We sold your car, which was necessary, but don't worry, I'm all over getting you a new one with no payments and such. You'll have to get a new license plate, too, which I forgot to tell you the other day," she said and for the hundredth time since I started staying with Nicole I wondered if she was also having a bit of...fun with helping me out in my situation.

"Sure, but you know there's no rush with the car situation. Really, I have no where to go during the day anymore and if I want to get out, everything is pretty much walking distance and there's always a taxi," I said and Nicole nodded almost dismissively as we walked to her car.

"Of course, but since you're going forward with signing up to be a surrogate, you're going to need to get to appointments and such and I may not always be available to go with you, you know?" she said and I simply nodded. I was quickly learning that it was best to let Nicole talk until she exhausted herself.

"When will the agency get back to me anyhow?" I asked her as we got into her car and she pulled away from the house.

"It usually takes a couple of days at the most, they welcome applicants," she said and I nodded thoughtfully as I wondered how weird it would be to be pregnant with another couple's baby.

"I'll be starting another round soon, and it's gonna be my last time before I quit the program," Nicole said and I looked at her in surprise. I knew she was a surrogate, but I didn't know that she was going to be…impregnated soon.

"So…like when will you be…" she glanced at me and chuckled softly.

"Implanted? Next week, hopefully it takes, apparently this couple doesn't have all the money in the world and can't afford for the procedure not to work on the first try," Nicole said and I realized then that I had a lot of research to do.

"So why are you quitting after this next pregnancy?" I asked her and she looked at me as if the answer should have been obvious.

"Because I've nearly gotten all my loans paid

off and I want to preserve my body for kids of my own one day," she said and I nodded in understanding.

"Oh, I get it...yeah, that makes sense, I would only do it the once, regardless of how it pays," I said and Nicole smiled at me almost apologetically.

"Yeah, a lot of women do surrogacy simply for the money, but I also like the happiness it brings the couples, you know? These people who've been trying and trying and were losing hope in having a baby of their own, it's worth it to see their faces once the baby is born and in their arms," Nicole said and I sighed deeply.

"But still, it must have been hard to let the baby go," I said and Nicole shrugged one shoulder.

"It's something you have to mentally prepare for. Don't look at the baby as yours, think of it almost as babysitting, or safekeeping, you know?" she said and I nodded slowly.

"Yeah, I guess so…" I said slowly and

chewed on my lip as I continued to mull the whole surrogacy thing over. Nicole drove us to a really good steak house just outside of town and we spoke about normal things for once, like where we grew up and what we saw ourselves doing in the future. It was cool that she felt like such a good friend already after only knowing her at a basic level.

"Okay, so when we get back we *have* to have a Gilmore Girl marathon now that I know you love the show just as much as I do. It's definitely a Netflix night," she said and I giggled at her excitement as we walked back to her car from the restaurant.

"I'd kind of be confused if we *didn't* go home to watch Gilmore Girls after our in depth discussion," I said and Nicole laughed.

The ride home was filled with our singing along to songs on the radio like teenagers. When we got home, we both took pause at the sight of a Fed Ex truck on the curb and the dark figure of a man knocking on the door.

"I think that's my new phone…" I said slowly and Nicole nodded. I thought we both had the same immediate thought when we pulled up, that the man could have been Roland.

"I'll go and sign for it, stay in the car," Nicole said and I rolled my eyes, there she was being all guardian angel again.

But what if it *was* Roland? I wouldn't have Nicole deal with my problems. She got out of the car and approached the Fed Ex guy, I watched as she signed for the package and the man hurried back to his truck without a second glance and drove off. I sighed in relief and turned off the car before going to the front door.

"It was just the Fed Ex guy, and you have a brand new phone," Nicole informed me and I simply shook my head at her a bit fondly. "You go ahead and get that set up, I'll get Netflix going in the living room," she called once we were inside and she disappeared into the house.

I went to my room and activated my phone with the new phone number. I made sure to call the police station to update my contact information. Then I wondered how long I would be able to pay the bill before I at least got things going with the surrogacy program. I changed into a set of pajamas and then went out to the living room with Nicole who had also changed.

"You know, I think we just started the beginning of a beautiful friendship, you and I," Nicole said as I settled onto the couch next to her and I laughed.

"I think you're right; if there's a Gilmore Girl connection, then there is a true bond," I said and Nicole laughed.

We ate ice cream and watched about six or seven Gilmore Girl episodes before we both fell asleep. Come morning, Nicole had to go to her appointment at the fertility center and I was left in the house alone. I really didn't know what to do with myself for much of the morning and ended up cleaning a little and watching a lot of TV. Nicole had a cute house, it was all one level with an open concept for the most part. The living room was open to the kitchen and the dining room was adjacent to that. Through the living room was a hallway that led to the bedrooms and bathrooms. Just before Nicole got back, I checked my new email address on her laptop and found mail from the surrogacy program. There was a lot of information and instructions on what to do next, as far as moving into the registration phase of the program.

Nicole was right; I had to make an appointment at both an OBGYN's office and a fertility clinic that was affiliated with the surrogacy program. I got right on with contacting someone from the program to let them know that I would indeed go forward with registration. The woman I spoke to helped me set up my appointments. There was *really* no going back from then on.

"Think pregnant thoughts!" Nicole called out as she walked into the house and shut the door behind her. I laughed as she hurried to the couch and sat on it upside down.

"You know that doesn't really help right?" I asked and she shushed me.

"It worked last time, I'm sure it could work again," she said and I laughed at her determined expression. "Seriously, it's a process. Can you plug in my phone to the surround sound and play Mozart?" she asked me and I shrugged.

Everyone had their quirks, especially when it came to a person trying to impregnate themselves for the happiness of a hopeful couple. None of it was conventional, but it happened. I just had to come to terms with the fact that it would be me sitting upside down on a couch soon. Really, it was the only way out of my situation that made sense. I took Nicole's phone and plugged it into the sound system and found her Mozart playlist.

"Just to let you know Nicole…this is weird," I said and she cracked up into laughter.

"Oh, I know; don't worry, I swear this is as far as my weirdness goes," she giggled and I smiled at her and left her to her 'process'.

I was in the kitchen making a cold cut sandwich for myself when I heard a car door slam. Immediately, I tensed up and then peered outside and breathed a sigh of relief when I saw a girl walking from the car parked behind Nicole's.

"Is someone here?" Nicole called from the couch and I nodded and then remembered that she couldn't see me.

"Yeah, it's a woman," I said and Nicole straightened.

"Ah, that must be my sister then," she said and her tone sounded almost reluctant for some reason.

"You never mentioned a sister…" I said and I heard Nicole's sigh all the way from the couch.

"Yes, because she's fundamentally a difficult person to get along with. I slipped up and told her on a rare phone call that I was letting you stay with me for a while," Nicole said and then we both listened to her sister knock on the door.

"Did you tell her *why* I was staying with you?" I asked as I walked over to the couch so I could see her face.

"Ah…maybe some things had to be explained because of other things that slipped out…" Nicole smiled at me innocently and her sister knocked again. "Just don't let her make you feel bad or anything okay? I'll go get the door," Nicole said and paused the music before going to answer the door.

I really couldn't be upset with Nicole for telling her sister a little about her new roommate who was more or less freeloading for the time being. I heard Nicole speaking in a low voice with her sister at the door for a moment before they both walked into the living room. Nicole's sister looked a lot like her, though her hair was shorter in length and her features were a bit more handsome than Nicole's.

"Hi, I'm Ashley, you must be Alex," she said and struck me as polite, not like what Nicole had described at all.

"Ah, yeah, nice to meet you." I shook her hand and she smiled slightly and seemed to study me a bit.

"So...I take it you're staying with Nicole for a while? Free of charge?" she asked and I glanced at Nicole who rolled her eyes behind her sister.

"Well, of course, when I get...a job, I'll be pitching in around the house," I said and Ashley nodded slowly, her expression was almost as if she didn't believe me.

"And what sort of 'job' are you looking to get?" she asked me and I gestured to Nicole as I explained.

"Well, Nicole told me about surrogacy, and I'm starting the registration process for it," I said and Ashley gave me that slow nod again.

"But you do know that it could take weeks, or months even, before someone chooses you. *If* you get through the registration process all good to go and even then you don't get any money right away," Ashley said and Nicole sighed loudly.

"Oh, would you lay off of her. You know it isn't an issue for her to stay here until she can get on her feet, stop being such a ball buster, Ashley," Nicole said and Ashley practically squinted at me in suspicion as Nicole pulled me to sit down next to her. "Plus we spoke about this Ash, it's not your decision, or your problem," Nicole said, defending me against her own family.

"I'm just trying to look out for my sister, as you can imagine. She tends to have a heart that's three sizes too big, you know?" Ashley said and I caught that she was calling her sister naïve in a round about way.

"I understand. She's your sister and you have to look out for her," I said and Ashley nodded.

"I just want to make sure you won't be…freeloading off of her for like years or something," Ashley said and I shook my head no.

"If the surrogacy doesn't work out then I'll figure out another plan, I shouldn't be here for more than a year," I said and Ashley studied me before she nodded again.

"Alright then, so…what are you guys up to?" she asked Nicole who simply stared at her sister awkwardly for a moment and then gestured to her crotch.

"Well, I've just been injected, so I was doing my implantation process. Guiding an egg to my lining," Nicole said and I tried not to smile. She was trying to make Ashley uncomfortable that was for sure.

"I was around for your first 'process' remember? Maybe I'm good luck. Go ahead and get upside down, where's the Mozart?" Ashley asked and Nicole sighed.

"Well, I guess you're right…and I paused it over there," Nicole said and I remembered my sandwich in the kitchen.

The rest of the day was spent sending Nicole good vibes and mostly trying not to say the wrong thing to her sister.

The following day Nicole offered to take me to all of my first appointments; first we went to meet up with a person from the surrogacy agency where I had to fill out a bunch of paper work before going to my appointments at the OB GYN and fertility clinic. I wondered if being a surrogate would always be so exhausting…

Chapter Four

Parker

After a couple of weeks thinking about and researching the entire surrogacy thing, I finally came to a decision. I was standing outside of my casino and waiting for my car to be pulled around when I saw a man pushing his son's stroller, though his son was in his arms and pointing to all the lights of the Las Vegas strip. I would do it, I'd go ahead and find a surrogate mother. Once the car came around, I all but sped home to get on the internet so I could start the process and find a surrogate.

Strangely enough, my mom called me as I was walking into my office at home. I sat down behind the computer and answered the phone.

"Parker, how are you? I haven't heard from you yet today," she said as I navigated to the surrogacy site I found earlier in the week.

"I'm doing it, Mom…" I said as I registered to

the site as looking for a surrogate.

"Doing what, hun?" she asked me and I took a deep breath before telling her.

"I'm going to find a surrogate; I'm registering for access to the directory as we speak," I said and my mom gave the most dramatic sigh.

"Wait! Don't pick anyone yet, this should be something you have second and third opinions on; you should call Edward, and I'm coming over," she said and I hardly had time to even take a breath before she hung up on me.

I shrugged and then slowly went through the database of surrogate mothers. I hadn't realized that I had been so engrossed with reading profiles until I heard knocking on the study door. I turned my head from the computer and saw my mom, Edward, and his wife Melissa.

"How'd you guys get in?" I asked and both Edward and Melissa laughed.

"Well, your mom has a button for the gate and a key to the house, so we just followed her lead," Melissa said.

She was a petite woman, blonde hair and light brown eyes. Edward was a goner the moment he met Melissa because of her sweet nature and inherent charm.

"Oh, so if anyone robs my house, Mom, I know where to send the cops," I said and she rolled her eyes as they all walked into the room and gathered behind my desk.

"So, first things first, we need to take the laptop to the family room, hook it up to the TV and get a lot of paper to make pro and con lists," Ed said and everyone got into motion.

Mom took my laptop and Melissa raided my desk for pens and paper. I simply let them take over and went to get snacks and stuff from the kitchen. We reconvened in the family room and went through probably twenty full profiles before we all started settling on a few candidates.

"Okay, so we have three women, one is thirty, another thirty-three, and the last is twenty-four. Automatically, I say go for the youngest one," Edward said and Melissa rolled her eyes at him.

"Yeah, but the youngest one…what's her name? Alexandria…she hasn't had any previous pregnancies. I'd go with someone who's had only one previous pregnancy," Melissa said and I looked to my mom for input.

"I agree, but I like the Alexandria girl, she has good genes. Look, she's a lot better looking compared to the other two girls. The thirty-year-old one I'm not so sure about, she's a photographer? Yet she's doing surrogacy, I think she's just looking for money to be lazy and take pictures," Mom said and we all looked at her in surprise.

"Sheesh, Mom, I thought you were critical of me," I said and Edward laughed.

"Well, I just want you to make a good

decision. Your child will be half whoever you choose to carry the baby. I want them to have good character. The youngest, she's studying to be a nurse, I bet she's just looking to pay her way through school by doing a noble deed," she said and I chuckled.

"Well, that's two votes for Alexandria…I guess I found a surrogate," I said and we all nodded slowly and kind of smiled at each other.

"So you're actually going through with this then…" Ed asked me and I looked at him steadily and nodded.

"I'm going through with it," I said and then sat forward on the couch to reach the laptop on the coffee table. I requested a meeting with Alexandria and a surrogacy agent. "There, it's done," I said and then studied Alexandria's picture a while.

She *was* beautiful, she had mahogany colored hair and golden colored eyes, which was rare and remarkable. Her features were soft and feminine. She had a gently sloping nose, plump lips, beautiful cheekbones, and naturally arched brows. Her jaw was diamond shaped and she had a slightly cleft chin. Her smile in the picture was friendly, but also a little sad, or shy maybe.

"Trying to imagine what your kid would look like?" Ed asked, snapping me out of my moment of staring.

"I think you'd have a beautiful baby," my mom said and then I started to feel a little uncomfortable with everyone staring at Alex's picture. I closed the laptop and disconnected it from the TV.

"Well, now we wait until I get into contact with her. In the meantime, how about we go out for something to eat?" I suggested and everyone agreed on going to a nicer restaurant at one of the hotels on the strip.

"So, I guess now is a good a time as any to tell you and Mom that…Melissa is pregnant," Edward said once we were at the restaurant and all eating.

My mom gasped in surprise, her face full of happiness though and I smiled at Edward almost proudly.

"Oh, congratulations!"

My mom got up to hug and kiss both Melissa and Edward excitedly. I hugged Melissa and Edward and then held him at arms length for a second.

"You've made me proud, Son," I said and he cracked up and playfully shoved my arm. "Here I thought it would never happen," I said and Melissa laughed.

"Believe me, it's what we all thought, but one day he woke up from a nap and said to me in all seriousness, I kid you not, 'Mellie, I want to have a mini us'," she said, mocking Ed in a deep serious voice. We all cracked up because that *was* something Ed would say instead of saying that he wanted a baby.

"Well, I did want to have a mini us…" Ed grumbled, he never liked being the butt of a joke, but loved joking about everyone else.

Melissa rubbed the back of his neck affectionately and just by watching them in that moment I wondered if settling down the traditional way was worth it. To fall in love, get married and *then* have a 'mini us' with the person you loved. I shrugged mentally to my train of thought and dismissed it, I caught my mom eyeing me and I smiled at her curiously.

"What?" I asked her and she shrugged.

"Oh, nothing. Now I can't wait for you to meet your surrogate, so that your child and Ed's can grow up together. Wouldn't that be wonderful?" she said and Melissa perked up.

"I can see it now, our kids running around together as close as you two are, they'd practically be siblings!" Melissa said in excitement and then she and my mother went into a whole excitable conversation about the future and babies. Ed and I then pretty much tuned into our steaks and let them talk until they wore out.

                            * * *

It took only a day for the surrogacy agency to
get back to me, and I made an appointment with a
representative to meet with Alexandria the same day
during the evening. I had to say I was a bit nervous,
but that was to be expected, this was a big step. I was
glad that Ed would be going through the same things
right there with me. We could maybe form an
expecting father support group or something; I was
sure those existed. While at work, I found it
impossible to sit at my desk, so I went down to the
casino and walked around to make sure the guests
were having fun, win or lose.

      "It's the legend himself! Parker Spesato, it's
been a while."

      I turned around with a rueful smile at the
sound of Benny Morricone's voice. Benny was
definitely a shady figure on the strip.

      He went under the guise of being an
investment broker and consulted many casino and

hotel owners to try and sell stocks and whatnot. But really, I knew that Benny's business was a front, a way to launder money from his real business. The Vegas strip had an ugly side that was necessary when large sums of money were being gambled. Benny was a part of that necessary evil to keep casino owners and their board members happy. Card counters, con men, and the like, were quickly taken care of once spotted.

"Yes it has, Benny. I thought I told you not to come around here selling your penny stocks," I said and Benny laughed good-naturedly.

He was a well kept guy; tall and athletic, clean shaven, sharp features, his brown hair was kept low in a crew cut and I never saw him around in anything less than a two-piece suit. His eyes were the oddest shade of grey, though, and they never missed a beat.

"You know I don't go around spouting that crap, Parker. Anyway, I came down here because...well, I need a favor, and you're the only guy who can really grant me this favor," he said, getting right to business.

"Ah, let's go up to my office, we'll see what I can do for you," I said and Benny smiled.

"Thanks for hearing me out, Parker, I knew you were a good guy," Benny said and I simply smirked and shook my head at him.

"Yeah well, I still haven't heard the 'favor' you need from me yet," I said and Benny chuckled as we walked over to the staff hallway to take the elevator up to the offices. Once we were safely inside my office, I sat behind my desk and looked at Benny expectantly as he casually walked around the room checking things out.

"So what's the favor Benny?" I asked him. I figured I'd at least hear him out. You never knew when you'd need the services of Benny Morricone, and if he owed me a favor, that only worked out for me in the end.

"I'm trying to catch a counter. But he's good and he hops around from casino to casino. If my predictions are correct, and they always are, I'd say he's coming here next. I need to make sure he never steps foot in the Grand, so I have to catch him now."

"So, if you were tracking him well enough to catch his pattern, why haven't you caught him yet?" I asked and Benny sighed.

"He's got a group, like that fucking movie that came out way back when. They never bet too high or win too much, but they are racking up quite a bit because they never lose," Benny said and that was the signifier; if a gambler never loses, even if he's betting pennies and winning pennies, it's to be expected that he's cheating the system.

"So, you want to have your guys come in here and set up a sting of some sort?" I asked and Benny nodded.

"Yes, but don't worry, whatever money he wins off of you guys you'll get back, of course," he said and I pursed my lips. "You've heard of how I work, Parker, it'll be just another day in the casino;

no one will be the wiser of me and my guys cleaning up that little crew," Benny said and I nodded slowly.

"Alright, but one stipulation…if anything gets messy the cops *will* be called," I said and Benny inclined his head.

"I respect that and I'll accept it as a part of our deal. Honestly, I'm so confident that my plan will run smoothly, *you* won't even suspect anything is going on." Benny said and I chuckled.

"Alright, Benny, I'm agreeing to the favor; you don't have to sell me anymore. Just know that if it's pulled off, you owe me one," I said and Benny grinned.

"Of *course*, I wouldn't have it any other way."

I stood up and rounded the desk as he walked over to me so we could shake hands on the deal.

"Excellent, I'll get out of your hair then, Parker. You'll see me again soon," he said before he winked at me and left the room.

After that, the day crawled as I was pretty much only focused on the surrogacy appointment after work. Six o'clock couldn't come fast enough and I was on the way to the surrogacy agency. The building was a huge facility. When I stepped inside, the guy at the front desk gave me directions to the matching agency and I forced myself to take deep breaths and cool it a little as I made my way to the matching office.

"Hi, can I help you?" The woman behind the desk in the contemporary, but comfortable waiting room called my attention and I walked over to her.

"Ah, yes, I have an appointment with Sadie?" I said and the receptionist smiled.

"You must be Mister Spesato. Can I ask for your I.D. so I can check you in and then I'll let Sadie know you're here," she said and I pulled out my wallet and she got me signed in and then made the call to Sadie.

I sat down on one of the sofa chairs and

waited until a short woman emerged from the hallway behind the desk. She wore big wire rimmed glasses and her greying blonde hair was pulled into a bun on the top of her head. She was definitely a quirky character, but then she smiled warmly at me and I had the feeling that she was one of those instantly likeable people.

"Parker, it's lovely to meet you. From our phone conversations, I knew you'd be a handsome one," she said and I didn't know how to react as I didn't expect the comment. The front desk girl groaned and I glanced back at her.

"I forgot to warn you, Sadie is a notorious flirt," she said and then I laughed.

"Oh, ignore Rose, come on back, Alexandria is waiting on us," Sadie said and I followed her down the hallway and into an office on the left. The room was comfortable and my eyes went immediately to the woman standing by the window and looking out. Her arms were crossed over her chest and her expression was thoughtful.

"Alex, this is Parker Spesato," Sadie said as we walked into the room and she closed the door behind us. Alexandria turned around and faced me. The first thought that popped into mind was that she was even more beautiful than her picture. Then she smiled and I wondered if I had gotten myself into another situation entirely.

Chapter Five

Alexandria

Parker was...well, he was gorgeous. He had that sort of chiseled jaw that models and a lot of actors had. He had a straight nose and soft looking inviting lips. His eyebrows were the kind that some guys had that made them instantly sexy. He had a scar running through the edge of one of them and they appeared to be as if he got them done or at least touched up. Then, of course, he had those long eyelashes and the greenest eyes that offset with his black hair perfectly. Then, just for overkill, he had to have a smattering of attractive five o'clock shadow on his jaw.

I forced myself to behave like a normal and intelligent human being and smiled at him before crossing the space in between us to shake his hand. "It's nice to meet you Mister Spesato," I said and he smiled at me warmly.

"Please, call me Parker. And I have to say it's great to finally meet you as well. I'm glad you were available so soon," he said and I chuckled.

"I guess it's fate," I said and he laughed lightly before Sadie came over and gestured us to the sitting area across the room from her desk.

"Yes, I'd say so. Usually, hopeful parents who look through the online directory and find the perfect surrogate are disappointed. The database doesn't specify if a surrogate is unavailable or not. It's just a list of who *is* registered as a surrogate," Sadie explained and sat down next to me on the smaller couch while Parker sat on the other couch.

"But, just so we're all aware here, Alexandria *is* a new surrogate, she's never gone through a pregnancy before and, of course, Mister Spesato, you are new to the world of surrogacy, as well. So we have *a lot* to talk about. I'll be explaining the process in detail, what's expected of you, Mister Spesato, and what is expected of you, Alex," Sadie said and I nodded and then took a silent deep breath.

This was happening, there was no going back. Sadie looked at me and then Parker and she smiled. "Wonderful, let's get started," she said and then got up to get a couple of folders and packets of information for the both of us. The meeting lasted about two hours and once Parker and I emerged from the surrogacy matching office, I felt a little bit like I was out in uncharted waters. This surrogacy thing was a whole new world.

"So, ah, what do you think about all this? Are you nervous?" Parker asked me as we slowly walked out to the front of the building.

"I am, equal parts nervous and anxious at the moment," I said softly and he nodded his head, his expression understanding.

"I'd be lying if I said I wasn't feeling a little bit of the same. But I'm excited though," he said and I looked at him curiously.

"How come you want to be a single dad?" I asked him hesitantly, I wasn't sure if that was too personal a question or not.

"It's just time...time I settle down and have my own family," he said and I nodded thoughtfully.

"I would never expect a guy like you to...do something like this," I said and he laughed.

"Yeah, well, a few weeks ago, neither had I," he said and I smiled and looked down at my feet while we walked.

"So, uh, I guess I'll see you again, once all the financial stuff is cleared, to sign the agreement, then I guess we're ready to...implant," he said and I chuckled at his expression. There really was no normal way to phrase that information.

"Yes, you will, it was a pleasure to meet you, Parker," I said and reached out to shake his hand again once we reached the front of the building. He shook mine and smiled, then we went our separate ways. Nicole was right on time to pick me up and she beamed at me as I got into the car.

"Guess what!" she said and I laughed at her excitement.

"What?" I asked and she pointed to her belly.

"I'm pregnant!" she said and I squealed in excitement with her.

"Yay! Oh my goodness, your couple must be so happy," I said and she nodded.

"They are, we had lunch today and we were all crying," Nicole said and I smiled.

If I could make someone that happy by giving them a baby, then surrogacy was definitely a good choice. While at our meeting, though, Parker did seem a little bummed when he learned that in Nevada, I wasn't allowed to provide my eggs to make an embryo. He'd have to go to a bank and look through even more profiles.

"So, tell me, tell me. How was it, what is your couple like?" Nicole asked me as she pulled away from the building.

"Well, it was just one man, his name is Parker Spesato and he wants to be a single dad…he seems really well kept and genuine I guess," I said and then chewed on my bottom lip as I rewound the entire meeting in my mind.

"*Parker Spesato*? Really?" Nicole asked me with disbelief in her voice.

"Yeah…do you know him?" I asked her and she snorted.

"Of course! He's only the owner of one of the biggest casino resorts on the strip! The Moondance! Parker Spesato is basically a billionaire," she said and my eyes widened.

"Oh my god…Well I knew he had money just from the way he looked, but I had no idea…" I said and Nicole gasped again.

"Was he gorgeous in person? His pictures are one thing, but I can only *imagine* what he looks like in the flesh," she said and I laughed.

"Calm down, Nicole, you're practically waxing poetic," I said and she laughed.

"Well, he *was* gorgeous wasn't he?" she asked me and I nodded.

"Yeah, he was…he really was," I admitted and Nicole gave me a knowing look and then we both dissolved into giggles.

"So, have you found a lawyer yet, you really should get a jump on that for when he's ready to sign the surrogacy agreement," Nicole said and I nodded.

"Yeah, he seems like he really wants to get things going. He seemed surprised when Sadie told him that he has to find a donor egg before we implant," I said and Nicole pursed her lips and gave me a sort of sly look. "What?" I asked and she shrugged.

"Nothing it's just…you know if he really wants *your* genes to help makeup the baby it can be arranged…" she said and my jaw almost dropped as I looked at her.

"What do you mean? This sounds like it's leaning towards something illegal," I said and Nicole shrugged.

"Well, the first couple I carried a baby for didn't want to use the wife's egg because she had genetic disorders that could be passed down to the baby. Then they couldn't settle on a donor egg and we met once and they asked if I would donate a few of my eggs to this specific clinic out of state. I guess some names were fudged around and voila, they ended up using my eggs," Nicole said and I actually couldn't believe it. She seemed like the *last* person I'd expect to contribute to anything illegal. Then again she *did* take me in initially for the excitement of hiding me from my ex. So, in a round about way, I guess I could see why she would do it.

"Well, that would really be up to Parker if he wants to go that route," I said and she shrugged.

"True, but you should mention it to him if he seemed disappointed that he couldn't use your eggs," Nicole said and I simply bit my lip and nodded.

Actually, I wasn't sure I wanted to carry a baby that was half…well, half *mine*, I think that would make giving it up too hard. "I mean, if this is all about giving someone the miracle of having a baby, wouldn't you want them to be completely happy with their baby?" Nicole asked me and that only further confused me.

"Nicole, you're reaching," I said and she shrugged.

"It was worth a shot," she said and I smirked at her.

Just then my cell phone rang and I answered it without checking, really there were only a few people who had my number, Nicole, the surrogacy agency, Parker, and the police station.

"Hello, Miss Frey, this is Officer Oden from the Paradise City Police Department, how are you today?" he asked and I couldn't exactly gauge the tone of his voice to interpret it.

"I'm alright, Officer Oden…ah—have you

caught Roland yet?" I asked him and he paused very briefly on the other line.

"Actually, Miss Frey, that's why I was calling. Roland is proving to be a slippery one to catch. There is still a warrant out for his arrest, but as for now we just can't *find* him," Oden admitted and I took a few deep breaths before saying anything.

"So what does this mean, Officer Oden?"

He took a breath before he answered. "It means you should be careful, but know that we are continuing to keep an eye out for him," Oden said and I sighed. I felt like he was telling me that there really wasn't much else to do for my case.

"Alright, um…thank you, Officer Oden," I said in a small voice and then soon got off of the phone with him.

"What was that about?" Nicole asked me curiously and I sighed again.

"Roland is in hiding apparently. The police

can't find him, but there's still a warrant out for his arrest. He's still out there," I said and Nicole looked at me apologetically.

"You shouldn't worry, he still doesn't know where you are, and has no way to track you down or contact you," Nicole pointed out and I nodded.

"Yeah, I guess you're right, I just can't help but to be a little nervous," I said and she gave me another sympathetic look just as we arrived at a building that read, H&M Attorneys at Law.

"This is my lawyer's office, he helped me with my surrogacy agreements. I was thinking maybe you can meet with him," Nicole said and I mentally shrugged. Why not, we were already there.

I consulted with Nicole's lawyer and he made some good points about things we should push for in the surrogacy agreement. Once that was all done, Nicole and I went to eat at a Mexican restaurant she swore was to die for. We spent the rest of the day together just like any two friends would and I couldn't help but love the fact that Nicole and I had become *so* close in such a short amount of time. She was like the sister I never had.

The following day, Parker called me around mid-morning and before I answered the phone Nicole begged me to put him on speaker phone so that she could hear 'the voice that came from a face such as his,' her exact words.

"Hey, Parker, how are you?" I answered and put him on speakerphone, rolling my eyes at Nicole's gesturing for me to do so.

"I'm doing well, Alex, how are you?" he asked, the simplest phrase and then Nicole was swooning in the seat across from me at the kitchen table. Parker and I exchanged a few pleasantries before he cut to the chase.

"So, I was able to get the financial logistics on my end taken care of and wanted to know when would be a good day for us to get the agreement hashed out and signed?" Parker asked.

"We can do that any time, I met with a lawyer yesterday and we're ready to move forward as soon as you are," I said.

"Great, my lawyer is ready to go as soon as tomorrow morning, so you just let me know when you and your counsel can meet at the earliest," he said and I nodded; Nicole looked at me pointedly from across the table and I remembered that I was on the phone and not in person with Parker.

"Yeah, yeah of course. I will," I said quickly and Nicole silently laughed at me and I rolled my eyes at her.

"I, ah, I also wanted to talk to you about this entire…egg donor bank issue. I'm having a hard time with it. There's just *so* many options to choose from and really I chose you because I figured I'd be able to use…well, your eggs," Parker said and then chuckled almost a bit nervously.

Nicole's eyes lit up right away and then she started pantomiming at me again. I knew she wanted me to tell Parker about what she told me the day before.

"Well, I can help you choose or narrow your search down if you want…" I said and Nicole rolled her eyes.

"I was actually hoping you knew of any possible loophole to where I could use your eggs," Parker said and then Nicole's eyes widened even further as she stared at me beyond pointedly. I couldn't help but giggle at her expression. "Was something about that…funny?" he asked me slowly and I quickly spoke to cover up my laugh.

"No, no, I'm sorry that was just my uh, my friend. She's also a surrogate…and she was telling me of a loophole of sorts yesterday, but frankly I have to let you know that it's illegal."

"Well, I'd only go forward with it once I know for sure this method is air tight, and of course, if you're comfortable that we use your eggs for the baby…" Parker said and Nicole gestured for me to put him on hold.

"Ah, um—can you hold on for a second, Parker?" I said and after he said yeah, I muted the mic. "What is it? You look like you're going to...I don't know, have an embolism," I said and Nicole gave me a bland look.

"Do you even know what an embolism is?" she asked and I waved my hand to dismiss it. "Okay, yeah, just tell him that you'll do it. Can't you imagine? The cutest baby in the world will be created. I wouldn't kick you out of bed you know," Nicole said and I sighed.

"Nicole, then we might as *well* have sex and have a baby without him paying me for it. Surrogacy is...I just—I don't know; half the baby would be *mine*. Nevada has the law for a reason you know?" I said and Nicole sighed.

"What do you think would come from this if Parker is forced to use an egg from someone he chooses from a binder and doesn't truly want? He wants your eggs!" she said and I sighed again.

"Sure, Nicole, but…it's *illegal*," I said and she rolled her eyes.

"Everything was airtight when I did it. Let me talk to him, I'll give him the information he needs to look into it," she said reaching for the phone and I held it out of her reach.

"Don't think of it as giving *your* baby away. Remember what I first told you about surrogacy?" Nicole asked and I shrugged.

Would it be so bad? If it could be proved that neither Parker or I would get in trouble for using my eggs to grow the embryo, then I guess I could do it. I'd just have to pretend that we're using someone else's egg.

"That face looks like a concession, hand it over," she said and held her hand out for the phone. I took it off of mute and then told Parker I'd pass the phone over to Nicole so she could tell him about the crooked fertility clinic in Arizona.

The Final Chapter

Parker

Alex and I had just come out of signing the surrogacy agreement and we went out to lunch to discuss what would happen as far as her donating her eggs.

"So you looked into it thoroughly?" she asked me as she sipped from her strawberry lemonade.

"Yes, the people at the clinic are extremely careful and thorough. Of course, it costs quite a bit, but money is never an issue for me," I said and Alex nodded slowly.

"Okay...well, just tell me when to go there and donate and we can finally do this," Alex said, although there was some hesitation in her voice and I leveled my gaze on her.

"Alex, I don't want to do this if you aren't completely comfortable with it," I said and she put her glass down next to her plate of chicken tenders.

We were at a nicer restaurant near Moondance and I found it funny and endearing that out of all the things she could order, she chose chicken tenders.

"It's something you really want, Parker, and I want to help you have your baby, so…I'm okay with it. As long as you're happy," she said selflessly and I smiled at her gratefully.

"Thank you, Alex. I swear you'll never have to do anything illegal on my account ever again," I said.

Yeah, I felt like a bit of a douche for putting her in the position I did. But I had sold myself on the thought of having a baby with her genes in the mix, not anyone else's.

"You're welcome…" she said and smiled at me sweetly.

Then she turned her attention to the chicken tenders and used a fork and knife to eat them. Yet another endearing quirk. Alex's brown hair fell from behind her ear, covering a portion of her face and

389

almost instantly my fingers itched to brush it back. But she took care of that herself.

"Do you think it will be weird for you?" I asked her, out of the blue. I just needed something to talk about instead of staring at her with the risk of my thoughts taking a definite turn.

"What?" she asked me curiously and I gestured to her stomach.

"Being pregnant, do you think it'll be weird?" I asked and she nodded.

"I just keep thinking about having the big belly. I know *that* will definitely be weird, but I'm sure I'll get used to it," she said and I sat back in my seat.

"So, if you don't mind me asking, what made you want to be a surrogate?"

Alex glanced away briefly and licked her lips. It was a nervous gesture, I saw that much, but of course, my eyes were then drawn to her lips and stayed there for a fraction too long.

"Well, Nicole told me about it and, I won't lie, the money was a big factor. But the more I thought about it, the more I figured why not give a couple, or a person, a baby if they have no other way to do so and really want a child. I guess…the gratification at the end is also a bit selfish…" Alex said and trailed off as she thought about it.

"You're giving a gift to a complete stranger, I don't think that's selfish at all," I said and she smiled at me shyly.

I imagined myself smiling back and leaning over the table to kiss her and then immediately wondered what the hell was wrong with me. It was unethical enough that I was insisting on using her eggs, but it was beyond the ethical realm to be attracted to my surrogate. That just complicated things…even further.

"So when is the appointment for me to donate?" she asked and I was glad she steered the conversation back to a proper course.

"It's in two days actually, I can text you the information, or email it, or both…whichever you prefer," I said and she gave me a small amused smile.

"A text is fine, it's better than an e-mail actually," she said and I nodded.

"Okay, great," I said.

The rest of lunch was spent with our exchanging small talk and such. Both Alex and I shied away from any more personal questions. After we ate, we went our separate ways and I was actually a bit anxious for Alex; I wanted to be with her for the egg donation, as well as everything else. But I wasn't allowed to be there when she donated, as to not raise any suspicion. Then, once she donated the eggs we had to go to a specific fertility clinic in Paradise where they don't check the eggs to see if they belong to the surrogate, they simply check the embryos, once the egg is fertilized, for any genetic disorders, if requested.

My phone rang as I was driving to the strip to pick up a document from the casino; it was Benny.

"What can I do for you Benny?" I answered; his plan *had* worked the other day. If he even had anything go down at all. I checked the security cameras and it simply looked like activity went on like normal. Though I did catch a couple of Benny's guys escorting someone out, they were dressed as security and I knew they weren't any of my guys.

"I have your chips as promised, they'll be delivered to the casino in the mail," Benny said and I had to admit that Benny sure did have all his bases covered.

"Alright, I'll look out for it Benny."

"It was a pleasure doing business with you, Parker," he said and we ended the call soon after.

Almost immediately, I got a call from my mom.

"Well? How did it go? What is Alexandria

like?" my mom asked and I smiled at the spirit I heard in her voice. She didn't sound as sad as she was even a week ago.

"Alex is...she's great, she really *wants* to give me a baby. She's kind and sweet...and...ah, yeah, she's great. I think we chose well," I said and stopped myself from waxing poetic about Alex.

"You're already calling her by a nick name?" my mom asked curiously and I rolled my eyes, of course she'd look too deep into things.

"Well, her name is a mouthful and she said it was okay that I call her Alex. Plus we're going to be quite close for the next nine months so I figured it would be weird if I called her Alexandria up until she's pushing the baby out," I said and my mom made a disapproving grunt on the other line.

"Well, you don't have to be so smart with me, Parker, all I did was ask a question," mom said and I sighed softly.

"I'm sorry, Mom, I'm just a little edgy. I'm

anxious for the whole implanting thing to be done and over with," I said to cover up my defensiveness.

"I understand, Parker, but you have to take a breath. You have your surrogate and you have an agreement signed, it's happening. Relax," she said and I took a deep breath.

"You're right, Mom. Well, I have to run into the casino for a second, I'll call you later," I said and we ended the call.

Once I pulled up to the casino, I texted Alex the information she needed and told her to keep in touch so that I knew how everything went. I knew I'd be anxious up until she was actually implanted. After I took care of the errand at the casino, I met up with Edward for a quick beer before dinner.

"Yo, Parker, you look stressed," Ed said as I got to the bar near his house.

I sat down next to him at the counter and he patted me on the back.

"I'm just…I don't know, keyed up you know?" I said and Edward nodded.

"Makes sense, I mean you're about to get your surrogate implanted, and then she's going to be giving you a baby after nine months," Ed said and I nodded. "I mean, when Melissa told me she was pregnant, even though I wanted the baby, I got so nervous. I was freaking out for, like, a day. It's not even like we aren't all together financially or don't have space in the house, or anything like that. We're set, we have nothing to worry about apart from *raising* the baby," Ed said and that only made me feel that much more stressed.

"And I'm an idiot, that didn't make things better at all did it?" Ed said and then he motioned for the waiter. "Can I get a round of your best beer please?" he asked the bartender and I sighed deeply.

"It's fine, Ed, I haven't reached *that* level of worry yet. It's just that…well, technically, Alex and I aren't supposed to be using her eggs to make the embryo," I said and Ed quirked an eyebrow at me.

"So what, you're stressed about choosing from the donor bank?" Ed asked and I shook my head.

"No, I, ah…well, I figured out a *way* to get around that," I said and Ed looked at me with raised eyebrows.

"*Really*? Like what kind of 'way'?" Ed probed and I shrugged.

"Like, a slightly bent outside the law sort of way," I said and Ed actually laughed at me and clapped me on the back a few times.

"That's fantastic man, do what you have to do. It's *your* baby, and Alex is freaking hot," he said and I nearly punched him.

"Dude, Melissa?" I asked and Ed grinned at me boyishly.

"She's the absolute love of my life, but I have eyes, Parker," Ed said and I just shook my head and then closed my hand around the glass of beer the bartender finally set in front of me.

397

"I guess…" I grumbled and Ed gave me a weird look before he picked up his own beer and took a drink.

"So, when do you have to go and put *your* stuff in a cup?" Ed asked me and I nearly choked on my beer and he laughed.

"What the hell man? What kind of a question is that?" I asked and Ed simply kept laughing.

"I had to lighten the mood somehow!" he said and then laughed again.

"You're such an idiot," I said and shook my head with a smirk.

* * *

About a week later, I was sitting in the waiting room of the fertility clinic with Alex and I was pretty sure we were equally nervous. She was wearing a casual skirt that fell down to her knees and a fitted shirt with long sleeves. It was not helping my nerves any that she looked so enticing; her legs were long and it was clear to see how perfectly round her breasts were.

"Ah, can we talk about something? I'm kind of nervous," she said and I sat forward in my seat. We were waiting to be called back by a nurse.

"Sure, yeah…um…what are you going to do after this?" I asked her and she gave a short laugh and then shrugged.

"I don't know, Nicole has this ritual she does where she listens to Mozart and sits upside down on the couch. Apparently, it's a sure thing for the embryo to attach…" she said and then trailed off and gave me a shy smile.

"Anything that'll help, I'm on board for," I said and then Alex ran her fingers through her hair to brush it out of her face. It looked so silky, then she was looking at me with her golden eyes and smiling slightly and pointing to what I was wearing. With her long legs folded all ladylike underneath the chair and her shirt clinging to her skin, I wanted to take her home and make a baby the old fashioned way.

"I've never seen you out of a suit before. The jeans look good on you," she said with that shy smile and I chuckled briefly.

"Yeah well, I figured I'd take the day off. Maybe I can be there when you do your friend's ritual," I suggested and Alex laughed almost nervously and shook her head slightly.

"No, it's alright, but I'll definitely let you know when I start taking the pregnancy tests," she said and I nodded.

"Oh, alright…that works too," I said and then the nurse stepped out into the waiting room and called Alex's name. "Can I come back with you?" I asked and she nodded.

"Of course you can," she said and I followed her back.

The nurse took us back to a procedure room and explained everything to Alex that would happen.

Then Alex was given a gown to change into and I stepped out of the room until the doctor came around and I followed him back inside. A nurse followed us with an ultrasound machine and I became more curious than anything about the entire process.

"So, are we ready?" the doctor asked with a smile and I looked over at Alex, she was sitting perched on the examination table and she put on a brave smile and nodded.

"Definitely, let's get those babies in me," she said and the nurse chuckled.

"Great, it's always helpful to be positive," he said and I walked over to the table with him and stood next to Alex.

He directed her in how to lie back and she actually reached out for my hand as the nurse got the ultrasound ready and placed a blanket over her belly and the tops of her legs. The doctor got this syringe and long catheter looking thing ready. Alex and I had decided to only go with two in case both attached, but also in case one didn't another one might go through. I wasn't too worried about the embryos failing to attach; yeah, it was an expensive procedure, but I could afford to try again.

"Alright, just take a deep breath and…" the doctor directed Alex as he put the catheter in her and she inhaled deeply and held on to my hand firmly.

The nurse handled the ultrasound and held it on Alex's belly as the doctor watched the screen and guided the catheter into her uterus. The process was relatively quick, I focused on Alex's face as she gazed up at the ceiling almost curiously while the doctor did his thing.

"And there we go, perfectly positioned," the doctor said with a wide smile and Alex turned her head to look at the ultrasound screen, her eyes wide with curiosity and bit of wonder.

"That was fast…" I said when the doctor slowly took the catheter out of Alex.

"Yep, IVF is much more successful with an

ultra sound guided transfer. And I've done it so many times that it takes no time at all to do," the doctor said and then smiled at Alex as he put the instruments away and the nurse cleaned up Alex's stomach from the ultrasound jelly.

"So that's it? Now we wait?" I asked him and he nodded.

"Now we wait. I'd recommend you come back in to take a blood pregnancy test in two weeks. But if you want you can take a home pregnancy test a little earlier than that. Though I have to advise that the home tests don't always give accurate results for IVF transfer patients," the doctor said and Alex nodded.

"Oh, okay then…" she said and then the doctor gave Alex some more advice in what to do during the next couple of weeks and that was that.

"So um…I can give you a ride home if you like. Or maybe we can go and get something to eat before you go home," I suggested. Alex and I had met at the clinic and I wanted to spend some more time around her.

"Ah, actually Nicole is picking me up and then we're going to go home..." she said evasively and I wondered for the first time if she was hiding something from me about her life at home.

"Oh, all right then, so...you'll call me if you need anything?" I asked her and she nodded.

"Yeah, definitely," she said and then I gave her a brief hug.

It felt so incredibly *right* to have her in my arms that I was left speechless with confusion. She waved to me after our hug and then stepped out of the office. I took several deep breaths before I left to go visit with my mom, Ed, his dad, and Melissa, who were over at her place.

THE END

Authors Personal Message:

Hey hey hey!

I really hope you enjoyed my novel and if you want to check out all my other releases then just head to my Amazon Page and see them all!

Also, I would really love if you could give me a rating on the store using the below link!

Remember

Peace, Love & High Heels

Lena x x

Fancy A FREE Romance Book??

Join the "**Romance Recommended**" Mailing list today and gain access to an exclusive **FREE** classic BWWM Romance book along with many others more to come. You will also be kept up to date on the best book deals in the future on the hottest new BWWM Romances.

* Get FREE Romance Books For Your Kindle & Other Cool giveaways

* Discover Exclusive Deals & Discounts Before Anyone Else!

* Be The FIRST To Know about Hot New Releases From Your Favorite Authors

Click The Link Below To Access This Now!

Oh Yes! Sign Me Up To Romance Recommended For FREE!

A MUST HAVE!

TALL, WHITE & ALPHA

10 BILLIONAIRE ROMANCE BOOKS BOXSET

An amazing chance to own 10 complete books for one LOW price!

This package features some of the biggest selling authors from the world of Billionaire Romance. They have collaborated to bring you this super-sized portion of love, sex and romance involving loveable heroines and Tall, White and Alpha Billionaire men.

1 The Billionaire's Designer Bride – Alexis Gold
2 The Prettiest Woman – Lena Skye
3 How To Marry A Billionaire – Susan Westwood
4 Seduced By The Italian Billionaire – CJ Howard

5 The Cowboy Billionaire's Proposal – Monica
Castle
6 Seduced By The Secret Billionaire – Cherry Kay
7 Billionaire Impossible – Lacey Legend
8 Matched With The British Billionaire – Kimmy
Love
9 The Billionaire's Baby Mama – Tasha Blue
10 The Billionaire's Arranged Marriage – CJ Howard

START READING THIS NOW AT THE BELOW LINKS

Amazon.com > http://www.amazon.com/Tall-White-Alpha-Billionaire-Collection-ebook/dp/B0115KNSMA/

Amazon.co.uk > http://www.amazon.co.uk/Tall-White-Alpha-Billionaire-Collection-ebook/dp/B0115KNSMA/

Amazon.ca > http://www.amazon.ca/Tall-White-

Alpha-Billionaire-Collection-
ebook/dp/B0115KNSMA/

Amazon.com.au >
http://www.amazon.com.au/Tall-White-Alpha-
Billionaire-Collection-ebook/dp/B0115KNSMA/

Made in the USA
Las Vegas, NV
27 March 2021